THE TIME MASTERS

THE
TIME
MASTERS

by WILSON TUCKER

NELSON DOUBLEDAY, Inc.
Garden City, New York

For Brian

Prologue

HE FELL SLOWLY through a black and colorless vacuum which still lacked sufficient substance to be called a sky, a suited figure pinwheeling down in ridiculous fashion toward the planet below. A strange sun and even stranger stars turned about him in kaleidoscopic effect.

His ship had been hulled.

Not far away another body tumbled down with him, a lifeless exploded body hanging part way out of the gaping hole in the life-support suit. That other body had not been so quick or so fortunate, had not escaped the demolished ship with its suit and its life intact; his slow revolving glimpses of the corpse limned in sunlight revealed that the body had exploded instantly when it was thrown from the ship.

He did not recognize his dead companion—could not, really, but he supposed it had been some off-duty crew member caught in a moment of relaxation. Accidents were so infrequent that no one wore their life-suits all the time. The two of them drifted leisurely downward toward the nameless planet, a world enveloped in blue vapors.

Were there other survivors?

The ship was long gone, after plummeting past like a

spent but monstrous bullet, to burst into searing flame as it struck the blue-green atmosphere and cindered. There had been scant time to escape the vessel. The crunching thunder of a meteoroid ripping through the hull and creating havoc in the power room had made the warning bells a mockery, faint by comparison and quite useless as signal alarms. He had automatically zipped shut his life-suit at the first invading crash—a reflex motion instilled by long training—but not feeling a personal danger or consternation until a moment later when he spun toward his wife on the bunk. Between his first and second steps toward her the alarms had tripped and he knew a momentary anguish, fearing she would not close her suit in time; between the second and third steps the big ship had exploded at the seams, ripped apart by the backlash of sudden power unleashed at the stern. The meteoroid had hulled them in the most vulnerable place. The great starship was done.

Many of the people of the ship had been catapulted into space, to struggle for their lives amidst the debris and the spilled coolant from the drive motors.

He *knew* his wife had saved herself, *knew* she was still alive; theirs was an intimate marriage and they knew each other's futures. She had undressed and bathed, preparing herself for bed, when the crises came. His final glimpse of her had been of her body stretched out on the bunk, struggling to close her life-support suit. The invading meteorite had continued its unseen way—now perhaps on an altered trajectory—but the shattered ship had fallen like the lifeless hulk it was until it struck the planet's atmosphere below. He had watched it flare and cinder with a renewed hope, thankful for some kind of an atmosphere.

Since then he had lazily followed it down—he and that other lifeless body nearby. He closed his eyes to shut out sight of it. Where was his wife? Were there other survivors?

He sensed a thin layer of air about him and opened his eyes to discover a faint and faltering daylight. His suit was beginning to react to the tenuous atmosphere.

In the next glance he saw his lifeless companion again and turned his head away to look below, instinctively bringing his feet together so that the conjoint energy of the two metallic shoes would right him, would cause him to fall feet first at a controlled speed toward the planet. He did not know the sun nor the planetary system—he had traveled as a passenger in the ship, unaware of its location when disaster struck—and so the world below was an unknown mystery. There were both light and dark areas scattered over the rounded surface and he assumed land and seas; and though he strained his eyes toward the night side of the globe, he could find no illumination that might betray a city or other sign of civilization. Perhaps he was still too distant from the surface, perhaps an artificial illumination was of a low order.

Following hard on that thought, he clutched the belt about his waist that contained emergency provisions and turned once more to look at his lifeless satellite. Food on the strange world might or might not be a problem, but the question of suitable water was of paramount importance. The seas were useless without refining equipment; sufficient rain water could be hard to come by, and even then might not be too palatable. He would be wise to take the rations belonging to the dead man.

A shipwrecked man either lived by his wits or he did not live at all—and in these circumstances he knew no sense of guilt about robbing a corpse. He regretted the spilled coolant lost from the engine room when the power train was wrecked; that precious liquid would have sustained him.

The atmosphere was gaining substance and depth but still he continued to fall, keeping his feet together so that the energized shoes might increase his rate of descent. He wanted to be on the ground when the corpse landed, wanted to be in a position to salvage the rations. Below him the land areas were taking on sharp definitions and he calculated where he might touch ground; off to one side the setting sun kissed the waters of a nameless sea, and he began searching the shoreline.

He thought again of his wife, wondering where she was, wondering where she was falling *now*, and wondering if they would find each other again on the world below his feet. Were there other survivors? Would he be able to find any of them? It would be like hunting a lost traveler in a vast jungle, a castaway on an uncharted island. The planet seemed very large as he fell toward it.

After an unclocked length of time he forced his feet apart to slow his fall, and ballooned his suit to cushion the landing jar. He was descending on a sandy, desolate shore.

Chapter 1

CUMMINGS, just in from Washington, folded his hands over the thick sheaf of typed papers lying on the desk and let his attention stray to the patch of sunlight spilling in the window. It was a warm summer sun and the window was open, letting in the mild traffic noises of the Knoxville streets. Cummings seemed to be absorbed in the patch of sun on the floor, studying the brightness of it, measuring its incredibly slow movement. The hasty flight from Washington had upset him, disturbed his heart and his stomach as flights always did, and he sought comfort in the warm splotch of light. The sunlight alone seemed peaceful, undisturbed and familiar.

The second man in the small office held his silence, waiting for his superior to speak.

Still carefully watching the sunlight and waiting for his body to attain a quietness, Cummings said, "It wasn't at all necessary to include that vacation request, Dikty. You know me better than that."

Dikty nodded, somberly agreeing with the supervisor.

"I know you. But I left you that loophole, just in case you wanted to put another man on. I hate to admit it but this is one time I've fallen down on the job." He waved a tired hand at the stack of papers on the desk. "I know all of *that* about the subject, and yet I know nothing."

"A tough one," Cummings said almost to himself.

"A tough one," Dikty agreed again. "I'm stopped. Everyone has to be born sometime, somewhere! But not this man—apparently."

The supervisor's responding smile was small and fleeting, entirely lacking in humor. It had been a quickening of the lips and nothing more. "I appreciate that last."

"Another loophole," Dikty explained uselessly. "I'm assuming he *was* born." A trace of bitterness crept into the investigator's voice. "I've seen the man with my own eyes and therefore I *know* he exists. And I don't subscribe to any of those theories and stories regarding storks, cabbage leaves or bulrushes. The man *must* have a set of parents, *must* have a flesh-and-blood point of beginning in space and time." He opened the palms of his hands in despair. "But where? The subject simply appeared—*pop!*—on a day and year, and has existed since."

Cummings continued to examine the pool of sunlight, moving his folded hands idly over the typed reports.

"What was the day and year?" he asked.

"March 8th, 1940."

The supervisor closed his eyes. Dikty, watching him fancied a shadow of an expression had swiftly crossed his face, and he wondered if the pain were a physical or mental one. After a moment Cummings spoke.

"Does that date mean anything to you?"

"Beyond being the birthday of my grandson, no."

Cummings hesitated a moment before replying, wrestling with either his thoughts or his stomach. "March 8th, or thereabouts, was one of the birthdays of hell on earth. You could also consider it *our* birthday in a manner of speaking; at least, the tentative plans for a secret security police went on paper at that time. On or about March 8th, 1940, the President set up the National Defense Research Committee; both the Manhattan District and our organization grew out of that."

"I had always thought Manhattan was the beginning," Dikty said absently.

"No." Cummings opened his eyes again to see if the pool of light had moved. "Another one of those eternal committees came first, in 1939. I forget the name. It didn't amount to much because it was hampered by lack of funds and lack of support in the right places, but *it* was the beginning of hell. Our Research Committee grew out of that in 1940, and the Office of Scientific Research and Development grew out of *that* in 1941. Finally the Manhattan District sprang from them all, in 1942." He sighed. "And there we are with more birthdays than you can count; I sometimes don't blame the public for being confused with Washington's confusion."

"Which would you say was *the* birthday?"

"Which indeed?" Cummings shrugged his shoulders and almost lifted his eyes from the floor. "It all depends on which date you prefer to observe—if any. The first atomic bomb explosion occurred out there on the desert in July, 1945. But the men responsible for that one regard the real birthday as three years earlier."

"Three?"

Cummings nodded. "Those men obtained their first real chain reaction in December, 1942. They want that recognized as hell's birthday. Personally, I don't know if the date should be carved in stone and worshiped, or thrown away and forgotten. I think it is the worst step in progress since gunpowder. Oh, well." He at last moved his eyes from the floor to stare at his assistant. "What most concerns us now is March 8th, 1940. The subject under surveillance first appeared on that date."

Dikty added, "Apparently."

"Yes, apparently."

"He came here to Knoxville about two years later," Dikty continued after a moment. "And I do know what that date means. When the first engineers walked out into the hills west of here to survey the site for Oak Ridge, our subject had already appeared on the scene and opened an office." Then he added bitterly, "He calls it an office. Just a couple of blocks from this spot, if you please."

Cummings smiled again, a faint trace of genuine humor turning the corners of his lips. "I appreciate that, too. I wonder if you do?"

"That he located so close to us?"

"That somehow he anticipated us again. We didn't get here until several months later, until ground had already been broken on the Ridge. But study the over-all picture, the places and dates as a whole. On or about March 8th, 1940, three things happened—besides the birth of your grandson. One, the powers-that-be in Washington decided in earnest to build an atomic bomb and began pouring important money into research. Two, those same powers realized the need of a highly secret security force to guard the bomb, and to guard the guards of the bomb—a hidden wheel within the wheel. And, finally, three, our subject makes his first recognizable appearance in public. Day and year, all three items. It occurs to me therefore that he might have known of the events of March 8th in advance, and timed his appearance accordingly."

"But he was located in Miami on that date," Dikty protested.

"To that you should have added, *apparently*. To be precise, he was found in Miami on March 8th of that year; he purchased a car and applied for a license, and so established himself for scrutiny. It has been difficult, I know. I'm mildly surprised those fuzzy bureaucrats have kept old records for more than thirty years, but we must thank them for that. But no one has been able to discover a trace of him *before* that purchase."

"That's correct, and that's where everybody fell down. There isn't *any* kind of trail prior to that date—prior to thirty years ago. *I* know, *I* went down there to satisfy myself." The strong bitterness had returned to his voice.

"So we know," Cummings continued, "that he was in Florida on the same day that historic events transpired in Washington. Very well. Eventually our subject wanders into Tennessee and opens an office here in Knoxville, shortly before the government begins building Oak Ridge twenty-some miles away. We see that it has taken him two years to drift the distance from Florida; he certainly has little regard for time, hasn't he? There is nothing really alarming about those facts when considered out of context, is there? Which is why I say he somehow anticipated us again. He arrived before we did, to allay suspicion."

Dikty slouched in his chair, staring through the open window. "The entire line of reasoning is rather fantastic."

"Agreed." The supervisor nodded slowly, his gaze lingering for a space on the sunlight brightening the floor. "And so you can tear up that formal request for a vacation. I realize what you've run up against and I appreciate what you've been able to do. Tell me about the man."

Dikty hauled an old pipe out of his coat pocket and pointed the stem at the desk. "It's all there in—"

"I don't want to read about him. I want to hear your version of him, impressions and opinions and all." He thumped the papers with locked hands. "This is the dry way of telling it, this is the formal way you dictated it to Hoffman. I'd rather listen to your emotions paint in the colors. Tell me about the man."

The assistant said hesitantly, "He saved my life."

"Yes. And so you will color him. I want to hear that."

Dikty packed and lit the pipe, sending great clouds of smoke churning toward the ceiling.

"It was about a year and a half ago—we had just cleaned up that McKeown business, remember? My wife and the grandchildren were coming in on the train and I was late to meet them; I suppose I'd tarried too long over lunch and didn't realize how late it was getting until I heard a train whistle." Dikty paused, the memory strong in his mind. "As I ran out of the restaurant I saw a taxi parked about half a block away, and I made for that. I remember thinking that if the cabby took the short cuts and cheated on the red lights, we could get to the station in time.

"I was—oh, fifty or sixty feet from the cab when I first noticed the woman, an ordinary sort of woman with bundles in her arms. She was running for the same taxi and with a determination to beat me to it. I didn't have a gallant spark in me—I wanted that cab and I wanted to reach the railway station in a hurry, so I continued running. I'd have made it, too—to the cab that is—if *he* hadn't stepped in front of me. I blinked, I suppose, and there he was, right in my path. I threw out my hands to keep from colliding with him and he had done the same—for a second or so we stood there, our hands and arms locked in balance with each other. I attempted to disentangle myself as quickly as I could, but he was rather clumsy about it; when I finally got free and stepped around him, the woman was entering the taxi. It sped away from the curb."

"And?" the supervisor suggested.

"That cab rocketed away from the curb and smashed into a gasoline truck at the next intersection. Both vehicles went up in flames."

There was a small silence in the office. The pool of sunlight had shifted its position on the floor as the sun continued its westward journey, and the early afternoon traffic of the streets was lighter. Outside the closed door of the room a stenographer's typewriter was busy. That was the only sound for long moments.

"And our subject?"

"I have no idea," Dikty supplied. "As soon as I could move after the crash, I ran back to the restaurant to call the fire department. When I returned to the scene I thought to look for the man but he wasn't there. I must have stayed there fifteen or twenty minutes before I again remembered my wife. I took another cab—with instructions to drive slowly—and met her at the station. She was crying."

"Crying?"

"Yes. There was something odd in her behavior when she saw me and our reunion was rather—affectionate. Quite some time afterward I found out why. The night before coming home she had dreamed of my death; it seems that I was killed in an automobile accident. And you see, when I was late meeting the train, she thought . . ."

Cummings nodded. "Yes."

"Well—that was my introduction to the subject. I never saw him again until a few months ago, when I received your instructions to investigate him. The name meant nothing to me so I started in the routine manner. He maintains a small office in that building down there," Dikty pointed through the open window, "and seems to have a small amount of business. He doesn't advertise himself as a private detective or anything so melodramatic. His office door merely contains his name and the word, *Investigations*. He has the proper credentials from the police; he did not apply for a permit to carry a gun; and he has never been involved in any unsavory situation since he arrived here almost thirty years ago. The police haven't a bad word to say about him, although no one seems to be really friendly with him. He appears to be the sort of man who keeps to himself and obeys all the rules."

Dikty found that his pipe had gone out, and relighted it.

"When I first saw him, I remembered him as the man who had prevented me from reaching the cab. Up until that moment I considered the whole affair as a lucky break—for me, you understand. I had always assumed it was a fortunate coincidence that he did what he did—until I saw him in line of investigation. My convictions changed on the spot. I can't tell you why they changed, or what caused it, but as I studied his face I realized that he deliberately stopped me that day to save me." Dikty put his hand to his forehead. "But I can't explain why I think that. I just *do.*"

"I'll believe it," Cummings said.

"If I had met him in any other way, had happened across him on the street or in a bar, I suppose I would have reacted normally. I'd have gone on thinking our earlier meeting was a lucky break for me. I'd have bought the man a drink, pumped his hand and probably made a complete ass of myself. But because you had started me working on him my reactions were unexpected, and somewhat startling. Because he was a subject under investigation I leaped to the conclusion that our first meeting was *not* a coincidence. And that, in turn, made me realize what kind of a meeting it had been. He deliberately saved my life with—well, hardly malice aforethought.

"He is a tall man, three or four inches taller than myself. Well over six foot, I'd say. Wears his hair in a crew cut, light brown, almost sandy." Dikty glanced at his superior. "He looks like an Egyptian."

"What?"

"An Egyptian. Tanned skin as though most of his life had been spent out of doors; a strangely hardened or *old* skin as though he had been living on a desert or the windy plains. I found his eyes quite odd. The corneas are yellow. That is a peculiarity common to people in the Far East and sometimes the Middle East. It strengthened my impression

of an Egyptian. Physically, he's a fine specimen. Lithe—I'd
judge his weight at about 175 pounds, evenly distributed.
For some queer reason he gives the impression of speed in
his build, as though he were constantly poised for flight, or
had been a track star in college and continued to keep in
practice. Trim and fast, always alert for something.

"He seems to be a quiet, unassuming man, not married.
Drives a two-year-old car and lives alone just outside of
town on a rented place, a mile or so beyond the trailer
camp. Has a small house and a couple of acres out there—
nice rural picture except that he doesn't follow the pattern
set by the neighbors. No garden, no poultry, no livestock—
just himself and an apple orchard. He doesn't visit or en-
courage visitors. If he has any women friends, I haven't
discovered them. I've checked his mail through the post
office and he receives little or nothing beyond a mass of
technical journals and books. His evenings are as quiet
as his days—sometimes at the library, once in a while a
movie, occasionally just walking about town, but mostly
at home alone. Bookworm type. He is less a part of this
town than the people living in the trailers."

"You haven't mentioned his age," Cummings said.

"No—I haven't." Dikty stared at his supervisor, a wrinkle
frown creasing his forehead. "When he first made application to the police for his license, he stated he was thirty-
one."

Cummings nodded. "And today?"

"He seems to be thirty-one."

Cummings added in an ironic undertone, "Apparently."

"Tell me . . . Why our investigation? What started it?"

Cummings had returned to his study of the pool of sunlight. There seemed to be a fascination in it.

"That, too, was a routine thing," he answered finally.
"Someone discovered that he subscribed to every bulletin
and journal of science currently published in the free

world." Cummings waved a broad, sweeping hand. "Archeology, geology, astronomy, meteorology, chemistry, medicine, nuclear physics, everything. It was that last which initially attracted our attention. Someone was checking the subscription lists and stumbled across his name on them all, down to and including a social journal for the atomic scientists. When someone noticed that his address was Knoxville, the routine began." His hard knuckles rapped the papers on the desk. "And you know the rest."

Dikty was still frowning. "Subject apparently has an overly healthy interest in science. All science."

"Subject's interest might even be an unhealthy one," Cummings retorted dryly. "And so we are continuing the investigation. I want to know the source of his income, so we are checking his tax returns. I want to know how he appeared in Miami without previous trace, so we are checking on all ships that put into that port on and before the day of appearance. And checking other Florida ports as well. I want to know what is behind the mysterious coincidence of those dates, so we will continue to investigate him. You stay on the job—stay on him." He sat up and abruptly turned away from the sunlight to lock eyes with the other man. "I have already assigned another investigator to the case. Here."

Dikty said nothing, awaiting clarification.

"That is no reflection on your ability or your work," Cummings said decisively. "I'm satisfied you have done all that could be done. But I'm also satisfied that the subject is aware of you and aware of the supposedly secret organization you represent. I can see no other way of explaining that taxicab incident. We will bear in mind that his intentions toward you—and us—are friendly, otherwise he would have let you go to your death. Take note that he made no attempt to prevent the deaths of the woman and the cabdriver—only you. But still, the primary purpose of our organization is to protect our atomic structure against all comers, so he must remain under suspicion and investigation. Continue on that basis; meanwhile a new investigator he does *not* know has been moved in. To approach him in a new way. I prefer that you and the new agent do not know each other—I don't want to run the risk of having the subject link the two of you together. If an occasion should arise when you must reveal identities, you will be cousins."

"My cousin?"

"Yes, that is safe enough. You have no real cousins."

"Very well."

"Our procedure from this point forward will be to determine how the subject knew those various important dates in advance. I'll start Washington digging into the scientific and political circles of 1939 and 1940. Something may come up to connect it all. I hope so."

"I'm sorry, but you are way ahead of me."

"In 1939 and 1940," Cummings sketched the outline for him, "only the President and a *very* tight little knot of scientific and political advisors knew the United States was speculating in nuclear physics; you know the degree of secrecy maintained on that score. But still, our subject appears in public view for the first known time. In 1942, only the President and a slightly larger group of advisors and planners knew that these Tennessee hills would be the future site of an atomic plant. So our subject appears here and opens an office—an investigator's office, of all things. Talk about your protective coloration! And finally, about a year and a half ago, an agent of a supersecret security organization barely misses an appointment with death. Again our subject is in the right place at the right time. We find now that he is overly curious of the sciences, follows their discoveries."

"He doesn't seem to age," Dikty said absently.

"How did he know of that historic birth in Washington,

in 1940?" Cummings demanded. "How did he know Oak
Ridge would be built out here, in 1942? How did he know
of your existence—and perhaps mine? Believe me, Dikty,
when I say this outfit is tight, I mean *tight*. We don't so much
as have an official name—we just exist. And not all of the
President's Cabinet members know of our existence—only
a few of them. We don't appear on *any* pay roll; money is
secretly siphoned off to us. We aren't responsible to any
government agency, only the next man in line above us. And
each of us, every one of us knows only a small handful of
fellow agents. We don't even know who is actually controlling us." Cummings bounded from his chair and stalked
to the window, to glare across the intervening blocks at
the tall white building down the street. "How did he know
of *you* and why did he save *your* life?"

Dikty shook his head worriedly. "I can't tell you."

The supervisor's fists were clenched behind his back,
knotted in an angry ball. "I'm going to find out!" he said
savagely. "I'm going to root out everything there is to know
about that man, all the way back to the hour of his birth.
If he was born! I'm going to find out why his eyes are yellow,
why his skin is hardened, and why he hasn't aged, why he
lacks a past, why he thought you were worth saving, why
he's here in Knoxville. I'm going to do more than that; I'm
going to find out why he's alive. He represents a threat that
I refuse to allow to exist; we will either discover exactly
who and what he is, or he may cease to exist. I'll tolerate no
half-mysteries about him!" Cummings paused in his tirade
and half turned from the window. "Has he seen you—since
the taxicab incident?"

"I'd like to say no." Dikty was uncomfortable. "I take a
deep pride in my training and my job, and under ordinary
circumstances I *would* say no, definitely. I've been extremely
careful in shadowing him. But considering the unusual abilities of the subject—yes, he has probably spotted me."

Cummings turned back to the open window and stood in the sunshine. His outward anger seemed to have vanished, and when he spoke his voice was soft, silken. His eyes sought out the distant office building.

"What's his name again! Nash what?"

"Gilbert Nash. An assumed name, I suppose."

Musingly: "Gilbert Nash? And he is *still* here, after all this time. Do you suppose he knows what is happening out there *now?*"

Chapter 2

GILBERT NASH WAS AWARE of the man's bewildered footsteps wandering along the corridor just outside, was aware
of the stranger's hesitancy for several minutes before he
actually paused at the door and put his hand on the knob.
The steps were slow and somewhat baffled, ill at ease, as
though their owner had forced himself this far but didn't
quite know what to do next—or couldn't make up his mind to
do it. They had faded away for some seconds as the man
drifted along to the far end of the corridor, and then they
returned to pause at last before his office door. The shape of
the bewildered man appeared only as a fuzzy haze on the
door's frosted glass pane. Gilbert Nash remained in his chair
and watched the indistinct shape, watched to see what it
would finally do.

The knob turned suddenly and the man darted in.

He stopped just past the doorway staring at Nash, looking
to see what a private detective would be like, looking around
the room without actually seeing it, still undecided what to
do.

Nash slowly got to his feet. "Come on in. I won't bite
you."

His voice was low, casual and pleasant; it sounded as

though the speaker didn't really care if the stranger entered or not. Whatever the bewildered man chose to do was acceptable.

The newcomer made a move to push the door shut behind him. "I'm—I came up to see you. My name is—is it quite all right? May I talk?"

Nash nodded, amused. "Quite all right. You are here with a problem. There is the same confidence between a client and myself as between doctor and patient." He reached out a casual hand to half turn an empty chair toward the visitor. "Come in and sit down."

The man was wearing most of his troubles on his timid face. It needed no second glance to reveal that he wasn't merely having domestic difficulties, he was drowning in the miseries. It was in his walk, in his unconscious slouch as he sank into the proffered chair; it hung from his shoulders like the unpressed coat he wore and it preyed on his mind constantly, spilling out over his face. He failed to see Nash's outstretched hand, may have failed to see the man himself very clearly. He slumped in the chair and ran a moist palm across his forehead, moist from things other than the mild summer heat. Knoxville in summer could be hot, but not that insufferable.

"I don't want this in the papers," the man said.

Nash smiled politely. "It won't be. Unless you've murdered someone."

"Oh, heavens, no!" His voice and his body had risen with alarm at the suggestion, and now he slowly dropped back into the chair, forcibly relaxing. "Nothing like that, oh no, nothing. It's my-my name is Gregg Hodgkins. It's my wife . . ."

Nash nodded. "Of course."

Hodgkins was well dressed but he wasn't so well pressed. He crushed an expensive straw hat in his hands and occasionally discovered himself worrying his twisted necktie. He wasn't a soft man by any measure; he possessed no paunch, his fingers were long and sure even though they were nervous now. His eyes were intelligent enough behind their blanket of worry, and his hairline was beginning to recede. He smelled pleasantly of a fresh after-shave lotion and the white shirt he wore was only barely beginning to muss. Hodgkins also wore a small *A-C-T* pin in his lapel.

"What about your wife?" Nash prodded gently. "Is she objecting to your work over on the Ridge?"

Hodgkins shot upright with sudden suspicion. "How did you know about that?"

Nash indicated the lapel pin. "I recognize that. I know that the American Chemical Trust runs the plant for the government, and I know that not every employee may wear one of those pins. You're some sort of a scientist out there; I wondered if your wife was objecting to your work."

"Oh . . . yes." Hodgkins fingered the pin absently. "Silly of me not to recognize the public significance of the thing. I'm afraid I'm not thinking very clearly any more. No, it isn't that. It isn't my work. My wife, she . . . Mr. Nash, you just *have* to find my wife!"

"Is she lost?"

"She ran away."

"Oh? When?"

"Less than . . . I'd say three weeks ago."

"Why?"

Hodgkins seemed to grow more miserable. "That's a long story, a very long story."

"All right. I'll listen—I've got all afternoon. You do want to tell me, don't you?"

The scientist sat up stiffly and stared into Nash's probing yellowed eyes while the words tumbled eagerly out. "Oh, yes, everything. I want to tell you everything, Mr. Nash. I don't know where else to turn. But you probably won't believe me. They didn't."

Gilbert Nash interlaced his fingers and relaxed in the desk chair, seeking comfort. "Who are they?"

"My doctor, and the company psychiatrist recommended by the doctor." He jerked out a crumpled handkerchief to swab his face. "I went to my doctor first from force of habit; I grew up in the habit of taking everything to the doctor, and he never failed me before." Hodgkins hesitated only long enough to risk a glance across the desk at Nash. "I could have saved myself the trouble," he added bitterly.

Nash almost folded himself into the chair, seeking the most comfortable position. His eyelids closed and his interlaced fingers were still. "The doctor said perhaps that you were imagining things? That you needed a rest?"

"Yes."

"And the psychiatrist?"

"He agreed with my doctor," Hodgkins continued in the bitter voice. "He sent me home. And I haven't worked for three weeks—that hurts, too. I haven't worked since she left me."

"The psychiatrist?" Nash prodded.

"He said almost the same thing as my doctor but of course stated it in a different manner; a mild neurosis, he told me, cumulative anxiety brought on by my exacting work and the attendant, continual pressures. Oh, he made it sound impressive, but mild and altogether harmless." Hodgkins paused again to look across at Nash. "I suppose it would do no harm to say I am in telemetrics."

"No harm," Nash agreed easily.

"Do you know what that silly psychiatrist said to me?" Hodgkins demanded. "He said I would probably be a very happy man in a matriarchal community, but that for the present there was nothing to worry about. And he sent me home from work; he comes around a few times a week to look in on me. Me—a grown man." He hesitated again. "And Mr. Nash, he reassured me that I am reasonably sane, as sane

as any man can be in *this* world today. I say that because I
can't be sure what you are thinking of me."

"Never mind what I'm thinking. Your work and mine are
alike in one respect; I don't form opinions until I've heard
the entire story. And if it is any comfort to you, sanity is a
legal term, it doesn't properly belong to medical terminol-
ogy." Nash nodded his head. "Please go on."

"Thank you." Hodgkins exhibited a minute measure of
satisfaction. "I need someone who can place faith in me, in
what I have to say."

Nash nodded again, still with a faint trace of amusement.
"And so you came to me."

"Yes. I read a great deal, both fact and fiction. And in a
vicarious way I believe I know the detect—the business of
investigation fairly well. I have a healthy respect for your
profession. I've come to look upon your kind as trouble
shooters, jacks-of-all-trades. Frankly, Mr. Nash, you are the
only remaining person I *can* turn to." He broke off again to
stare intently at the listening man. "Will you do me a very
great favor?"

Nash slowly opened his eyes to regard the scientist with
speculation. "If I am able—yes."

"Please"—the words were tumbling again, rushed and un-
sure—"don't laugh at me. Don't laugh at what I'm going to
say. I know very well my facts will sound silly and childish,
perhaps even fantastic, and under other circumstances I
might well laugh myself. But they aren't silly, they are bare,
bald *facts*, the only things I have left to cling to. And I
don't want you to laugh, no matter what you choose to believe of me. I don't want you to pat my shoulder and tell
me I am imagining things, that I need a long rest, that I
would be happy in a matriarchal state." He paused for
breath. "If you choose *not* to believe me, tell me so and
I'll leave. Refuse me—my case, if you so desire, and stop

right there. I'll walk out that door and not bother you again. But don't laugh at me."

Nash nodded assent. "That much is easily granted." He closed his eyes a second time and relaxed in the chair. "Where are you going to begin?"

"With my wife, with Carolyn. Everything begins with my wife—and ends there. The entire affair seems to be a complete circle of zero, our marriage, our life together; everything comes right back to here and ends where it began." He paused, summoning courage for what he had to say next. "She's too damned smart!"

With that he came to a full stop, looking for a reaction on the part of Nash. There was none. Nash remained curled in the chair, patiently waiting for him to continue.

"Have you ever had the misfortune to marry a woman far more intelligent than yourself, Mr. Nash?"

"No."

Hodgkins rushed on. "But surely you can imagine what a man desires in a woman. It has been said before by men more gifted than myself—an inspired chef in the kitchen, a patient mule about the house, a . . ."

Nash finished for him when he hesitated. "And a whore in the bedroom."

"Eh—yes. Among other things, the usual attractive physical attributes, a man wants a smart and very intelligent wife, a woman possessing sufficient mental abilities to understand him and his world. A woman who can stride alongside him, who can understand his problems and to a degree, help him solve them. But still—and this is a paradox, I will admit—a woman who is necessarily inferior to him, just a trifle inferior. A sort of delicate balance to the male ego. For a man also wants a woman who *needs* his advice, who must lean on him, who has need of his greater reasoning powers as well as his mechanical knowledge. That is the kind of woman every healthy man desires, Mr. Nash. I fully believed I had found such a woman in Carolyn."

Nash nodded again, seeing the image of Hodgkins's desired woman on his inner eyelids. He thought he knew what was coming.

"Just how old is your wife, Mr. Hodgkins?"

The question was met with a small silence, and when the answer finally came it was in an embarrassed tone. "I—we don't know really. She is an orphan, you see, and we were unable to locate the birth certificate. The situation stirred up a bit of a fuss when I first took a job with the laboratory people, as you can imagine. They delve into everything, but they couldn't find a certificate either. Carolyn and I finally agreed that she was about five years younger than myself —that needed bit of inferiority, you must understand."

"I understand. And you are . . . ?"

"Forty-six, now. So by our agreement she would be forty-one—we think. Sometimes I am not sure. She hasn't grown much older than the day I married her."

The yellow eyes snapped open to fasten on him. "What?"

"She never changed much." Hodgkins smiled with the memory of her. "I liked that, really. What man in love doesn't prefer his wife to cling to her youth and beauty? She was a handsome, striking woman on the day we were married, and still is. She could have easily passed herself off as being in the middle twenties then; today I would judge, she could get by very well indeed in the early thirties. Her youth seemed to cling to her."

"Did she use anything to maintain that youth?" Nash asked curiously.

"What do you mean?"

"Creams, lotions, the usual jars in her bedroom?"

Hodgkins was embarrassed again. "I don't know, Mr. Nash. We had separate bedrooms. Oh—I don't mean by that,

that we—well—but we always had separate bedrooms. She wanted it that way." He shrugged. "Offhand I don't recall seeing such jars around. I suppose she kept them out of sight. Carolyn was very tidy—marvelous wife and housekeeper."

"Yes, I can imagine." Nash's gaze lifted above the man's head and climbed the wall, absently speculating. "All right, she was your perfect companion. And you are a success in your field, in telemetrics."

Hodgkins fingered his lapel pin and nodded, unaware that Nash was no longer watching him. He began talking about himself, about his schemes and plans and dreams and desires during his college years; about the lean days that closed in on him after graduation when he first discovered industry *wasn't* waiting on the doorstep, begging him to work; about his frantic struggles to avoid the draft, and his subsequent hitch overseas; about his aimless drifting when he was at last discharged. He told the investigator about the day strange men approached him on an even stranger subject, and how he eventually found himself working in a concrete cell which was a part of many other cells, the whole making up a secret government organization called the Ridgerunner Project.

He recounted to Nash his later days, after he was transferred from New York to Oak Ridge and realized the meaning of "Ridgerunner" in the project. He mentioned in passing the journeys to the Cape to witness some of the rocket launchings, and his return to work with a new awareness of what *he* was doing, what *he* was contributing to the leap into space. And he told of the slowly growing strain of unhappiness between his wife and himself, despite his recognition of it and the striving to overcome it. He wanted desperately to wipe out that new strain for he remained deeply in love with her.

Hodgkins wound up by asserting, "I consider myself an

intelligent man, Mr. Nash. You'll grant me that, leaving false modesty aside."

"Easily granted," Nash said again. "But back to your wife . . . ?"

"Yes—Carolyn."

He lapsed into what was obviously a painful silence while his memory skittered back over those years, tracing again the days of his ripening love for her.

"In the evenings after work," he finally broke his silence, "I studied the technical books and journals I could not then afford. I had found a poor job clerking in a grocery store— it was the best I could manage—but I had never lost my high ambitions, my zeal to scale the heights in my chosen field. But I realized that if I waited until I could afford the publications it might be too late, and so I devoted my evenings to study. The larger libraries were splendid sources. Sometimes I was able to borrow from a university library, and frequently certain books could be obtained from state library systems. I studied hard, I tried to keep abreast of the field—and I met Carolyn. I discovered Carolyn in the library.

"Oddly enough, I first saw her looking at a schematic drawing in a radio magazine. She was tracing it with her finger. It startled me, and when I looked closer to discover what she was really doing, it pleased me. You must realize it was—and is—a very unusual thing to find a woman interested in such technical details. But she was. Have you ever read a schematic? It is done in two ways. Either you have a surface interest in the drawing and you follow each line from origin to terminus, with your interest being in that line alone; or you attempt to grasp the plan as a whole and retain the mental impression of each circuit, enmeshing it with the next circuit as you trace it. The end product is that you have a fairly cohesive picture of the scheme by holding the image of each circuit in your mind, meanwhile interlacing them all. I stood behind her chair and watched her finger; I don't know that she was reading the drawing as a whole, but I think she was."

"You couldn't judge by her finger?"

"No, of course not. The finger was merely a guide-post to the mind behind it. She went along splendidly for a few moments and then she seemed to run into trouble."

Nash nodded. "Yes, I was expecting that."

"You were? Oh my. Well—I don't recall at this late date what it was, but some difficulty arose that threw her completely from her train of thought. It may have been my presence behind her. And when you lose the thread of thought in a schematic, Mr. Nash, you may as well begin all over again. She was annoyed."

"I can well understand. Go on."

"Well, she pushed the magazine away with a little sound under her breath and started to get up. And I, like a fool, had to butt in; without thinking of what I was doing, I leaned over her shoulder to point to the trouble spot."

"You did as expected."

"I did?" Hodgkins was uncertain whether to be pleased or confused. "'Not *that* way,' I remember saying to her impulsively, and then I rather choked up and could say no more. She threw me one withering glance over her shoulder and I hurriedly left the library, in some confusion I must admit. She had created quite a disturbance within me."

Nash turned his bemused attention to the man. "Was it an act?"

"Do you mean, was she pretending to something false? No, I can't believe that. She was an utter stranger to me before that evening and I can't imagine why she would pretend to something, merely to gain my attention. I must remind you, Mr. Nash, that I was nobody at the time. I hadn't even a decent job. My clothing couldn't have been too acceptable." Hodgkins shook his head. "However, I avoided the library on the next few nights because I still felt some embarrassment over the incident, but less than a week later I had to go back. My studies were suffering—and the overpowering desire to see her again swept away any misgivings I may have had. The desire amounted almost to a pull, a compulsion. The memory of her continued to haunt me, disturb my days and nights, and I realized I could never rest until I was near her once more."

Nash regarded him silently and with calculation. He was beginning to learn vast things about Carolyn Hodgkins.

The scientist said, "I finally returned to the library . . ."

". . . and there she was," Nash finished the sentence for him. "You might say, waiting for you."

"Yes, really!" Hodgkins missed the intended irony. "I found her studying a book that I had turned in only a few weeks before. It dealt with a field closely allied with my own, can you understand that? It had not been easy studying for me, that particular volume, but there she sat almost swimming through it! I was both astonished and delighted! But still, I carefully avoided her that evening, preferring to sit in another part of the room just watching her—her profile was wonderful. Well, eventually the attraction of her body, her personality, overcame my reticence and I—that is, we—I don't quite know how to explain it," he finished lamely.

"No need to," Nash assured him in what he hoped was a sympathetic rather than an amused voice. "Easily understandable, it happens all the time. Mutual interest in your sciences, each of you obviously alone . . ." He let it hang there, casually watching Hodgkins.

"Yes, yes, of course. You do understand. So then I finally summoned the courage to approach her and introduce myself. She was not angry at all, she was most friendly." He closed his eyes for a brief moment of retrospective dream. "In time we became fast friends. We met again at the library several times, and then elsewhere; in a very short while I began entertaining ideas. I surprised myself, Mr. Nash, with the quickness and audacity of those ideas, for until then I had been something of a backward man half afraid of a woman's shadow. But you must understand, Carolyn's presence seemed to invite ideas."

"I'll just bet," Nash mumbled.

"I beg your pardon?"

"Go on with it, please."

"I thought," Hodgkins said after a small pause, "she was —or rather she would be what any intelligent man might call a perfect wife. The woman was beautifully endowed with everything I could possibly ask in a mate, including the remarkable intelligence I had always desired in my dream woman. A hundred enchanting little things came to light about her as we spent many pleasant evenings together. I had fallen in love of course. I still am. And I may as well make this brief, Mr. Nash. We were married." Hodgkins came to a full emotional stop, expecting some reaction to his tale. He got it.

Gilbert Nash stood up from the chair, stretched his arms lazily about his head and took a turn about the little room. He came back to stand beside the window overlooking the street, his back to his client. His voice, when he spoke, held a strange and muffled quality as though he were vocally hiding something.

"Hodgkins, can you stand a jolt?"

"A jolt? Well—I suppose so."

"All right, here it is. Just about any other man in the world who had his feet on the ground instead of in the air would know what happened to you. Quite plainly and frankly, you were taken in."

"Taken in?"

"Hooked. And if you aren't familiar with current slang, you were baited and trapped in a fine-mesh net. The net was that schematic drawing. But don't be alarmed"—Nash waved a negligent hand—"that happens all the time, too. A million women employ a million ways to catch a million men. Yours was the technical touch. Quite common, Mr. Hodgkins."

Hodgkins stammered, "I see."

"I wonder?" Nash asked under his breath. He remained at the window looking down into the street.

Behind him, half oblivious to any other presence in the room, Hodgkins was tightly wrapped in the warm memories of his wife. He had married Carolyn because he was madly in love with her, in love with her seductive body, her unusual beauty, her personality and her intelligence quotient, in love with the complete woman. Overwhelmed with love of her because she had noticed him and had not passed on, had paused to look. He was positive theirs was the greatest love since time's birth, all unaware that others without number thought the same. He had married her because he would possess something few other men could boast: an alert, brainy woman who was nearly his equal in any field he chose to explore. *Nearly.* He had married her because she could read a schematic drawing *but* encountered trouble on certain parts of it. That iota of necessary inferiority was present. He had married her because she would be a most valuable asset to his own standing and mentality. As she had been—for a time. But somewhere, somewhere along that golden line between the honeymoon and the ill day three weeks ago, the bubble had burst. Or half burst. He still loved her, if only she would continue to love him. *If.*

Nash turned around to find the man slouched in the chair, dreaming his dreams. "Which brings us to the present," he suggested briskly.

"What?" Hodgkins sat up. "Oh yes—the present."

"You're still married, still in love?"

"Yes indeed!"

"But your wife has walked out on you?"

"I'm afraid she has."

"Has this ever happened before?"

"Why—no. Not like this."

"What do you mean, not like this? Has she or hasn't she?"

"I mean to say, she took vacations—long vacations. Without me. She thought it best, you must understand." He seemed embarrassed at the confession. "Carolyn would go away for a time—perhaps two or three weeks, perhaps two or three months. One dreadful winter she was gone for seven months, and I was terribly upset. She—she said it was good for a marriage to have separations."

"Where did she go on those long vacations?"

"Oh, I don't know . . ." He paused. "Yes, I *do* know. She always returned tanned, deeply tanned, so it had to be Florida or California . . . the sunny places. She likes the sun and the sea."

"Did you ever attempt to trace her? Follow her?"

"Certainly not! She forbade it."

"And now she has gone again and you want me to find her?" He paused. "This isn't just another vacation?"

"Not—not this time."

"Are there any other men?"

Hodgkins visibly cringed from the thought. "I don't know. I don't think so. I've never seen them."

Nash felt a fleeting moment of wonder at the man's startling naivete. Gregg Hodgkins—scientist, scholar, valuable enough to be invited into the Ridgerunner Project, naive enough to be roped into marriage by a woman who carefully used his own special knowledge to lure him.

Nash said, "If your wife were only half as smart as you claim, friend, you would not see the other man. You never do, believe me; he's always standing behind your back.

But in the meantime there are some muddy points in your tale of woe which need clearing up. What was the cause of your separation?"

Hodgkins stared at him, sudden anguish in his eyes. The crisis had been forced upon him with those few words, a crisis he had clumsily tried to avoid all during his recital. Why had he split with Carolyn—or rather, why had she run away from him? The answer was painted on his face and written between the lines he had spoken earlier, but Nash waited for him to spell it out with hard words. What had caused the sudden separation after long years of married bliss?

"Because she had surpassed me!" Hodgkins cried at last, half ashamed to be admitting it.

"Surpassed you?" Nash prodded relentlessly.

"She was an unimaginable distance ahead of me! No, please—don't mistake me. I'm not mad, not angry. Jealous— yes, I'll admit to that. But I'm not angry at her for what she has done. Carolyn has passed me by! During all the years we have lived together, she sucked my mind of knowledge the way a vampire bat is said to suck blood."

Nash sat down abruptly to stare at the unhappy man. "What?"

"Everything I've learned in the past ten years," the man cried, "everything I've gained by hard work and sweat, Carolyn knew the next day! Will you believe me when I say she plucked from me every iota of knowledge I have, pulled it piece by piece from my poor head without my uttering a word!"

"Carolyn Hodgkins did that?" Nash reached out to grip the edges of the desk. "You say she pulled you back into that library with a physical compulsion, you say she hasn't grown much older than the day she married you, you say she takes separate vacations and you don't know where she goes, and now you tell me that she ransacks your mind of knowledge? Carolyn Hodgkins has done that? Your wife?"

Hodgkins nodded miserably. "Yes."

"Well!" Gilbert Nash exclaimed in mild wonder. "Well—finally."

Chapter 3

THE CORRIDOR OUTSIDE was fairly quiet with only an occasional passer-by stepping out of the elevator and clacking his heels on the hard flooring as he sped for some remote room in the depths of the building. There weren't many public offices on the seventh floor, one of the reasons Nash had chosen the location. He desired privacy above all else, despite his indicated profession, and the one room high on the seventh floor was ideally situated.

Nash stood at the partly opened window overlooking the city, overlooking the smallish cars and still smaller people crawling on the pavement below. The sunlight slanted past, leaving that side of the building and his single window in shade. Nash batted his eyes at the warm, sunlit city and turned about to face the room, his face an expressionless mask and his voice a flat monotone.

"Let's go into that more fully," he suggested.

"About Carolyn?"

Nash nodded. "About Carolyn."

"I warned you—you might laugh at me."

"I'm not laughing," Nash pointed out.

"Well, I've formed a theory."

"I want to hear it," Nash said.

"I'm a careful man—by training and habit. I must be careful in my work. I proceed on a theory someone else has assigned to me, following it to its ending whether that ending is a success or a failure. Or I formulate my own theories based upon previous knowledge and observation and then proceed in the same manner. I have formed a theory about Carolyn." He looked up, somewhat confused. "But you must understand I still love her. I do—to this day!"

"You love her. Keep going on the theory."

"In the beginning I didn't realize of course what was taking place; our marriage was too new, Carolyn was too new and I lacked previous data. I don't recall now just when I first suspected the truth. It was one of those years . . . One of those years I discovered that Carolyn was learning my most precious secrets, the most confidential government secrets that we at Ridgerunner were exploring. Ridgerunner was very strict, you must understand. *Nothing* was to be carried home to the wife and family, and following those dictates my lips were sealed. Never, never in the many years of our marriage have I spoken a confidential word to my wife—about my work, I mean. Not one word. I wouldn't even so much as mention the name of another man I happened across at the laboratory, for fear the mere name and presence of that man would partially reveal the particular experiment under consideration. You see, in our work, a man's name immediately identifies him with his subject."

"Yes, Newton and gravity, Heinlein and the moon. Keep going." Nash had again closed his eyes and was hunched in the desk chair, listening intently.

"So I *said* absolutely nothing to Carolyn about the work, nothing! But in a short while she knew everything I was doing, and everything I had observed others doing. I worried about it, puzzled over it, told myself I was deliberately fabricating false premises—but she *knew*, and in the end I realized that she knew. She would prove that to me when certain instances arose in my work that stopped me cold. I would stand still for days, unable to progress by so much as a single decimal point and in the meanwhile she would grow irritated with me. Impatient with me really, for I was holding her back as well. Finally her irritation and impatience would reach the point where she would drop some hint in our idle conversation. Not about the work stoppage, no, but she had the knack of inserting an irrelevant phrase or thought into whatever subject we were discussing. That irrelevant something would grow, in my mind, and in a day or so I would change it—that is, reassign the values, and apply them to the work under consideration. And immediately the problem would vanish, the knot would disappear and the work would go forward once more. And Carolyn's mood would change for the better. I have included all that in my theory of her.

"Carolyn helped me actively push my work, and in return Carolyn shared the results of that work. Against my conscious will. I puzzled a long, long time over the method she employed to gain access to my knowledge. Mr. Nash, the following is apt to be . . . to be . . ."

"Confidence of the client, remember? Don't worry about what it is apt to be. Just spill it."

"Yes sir." Hodgkins fidgeted. "At first—at first I considered mental telepathy, those Rhine experiments with ESP and that sort of thing. I wondered if Carolyn was—say sitting across the room from me and reading my thoughts; and although I blush to admit it, I toyed with that idea for quite some time and would find myself devising mental traps for her. I used to *think* things, sometimes revolting and horrible things—nasty little thoughts—and watch to see if she reacted to my thoughts. She never did, never gave an indication that she was 'reading' those thoughts or 'reading' my mind. In time, I discarded the theory of mental telepathy. That is, I discarded that particular theory of telepathy. Mr. Nash, I can't prove what I am about to say and so it must remain my theory only, but I believe I have discovered the channel of workable telepathy—at least between Carolyn and myself."

"I know one thing right now," Nash told him. "I guessed it by your manner and your growing discomfort. It is a rather delicate channel, isn't it?"

Hodgkins eyed him in wonder. "Very delicate. I've come to believe this telepathy of ours requires a physical contact. A very intimate physical contact."

"I'm anticipating you. But go on."

"This—I haven't even told this to my doctor—but as our years of marriage went by and I modulated my theory, I finally came to realize that we *must* have this physical contact for her to know my innermost thoughts. I've already told you that we maintained separate bedrooms."

He broke off to fidget, to glance with embarrassment at Nash. "I'm afraid this becomes very personal. I hope you will understand. In the beginning, of course, we were very much in love, always together, and incidentally unable to afford separate bedrooms. You've never been married, have you? Marriage begins with a maximum amount of *closeness*, of clinging together physically and mentally, of being constantly aware of one another and the desire to be near one another. But over the course of years that tends to wear away and you experience only periodically what you felt at first.

"It was during this latter period that I formed my theory of Carolyn. We had moved to Oak Ridge by this time, we could afford separate bedrooms. Will you—will you forgive me for this?"

"Easily done."

"I have formed the theory that Carolyn can know my thoughts by physical contact, that her mental powers are

limited to that means of conductivity. Let us assume that
we were holding hands—when you are in love, Mr. Nash,
there is much of that. When we were holding hands,
Carolyn could know my surface thoughts, could know what
I was thinking of in a vague, distant manner. When we
kissed, she was able to plunge deeper, able to read and know
everything I knew. I could feel *that*. I could feel her plumb-
ing my mind for knowledge. It amounted almost to a
physical probing. I knew what was happening and yet I was
powerless to prevent it. I was and am in love with Carolyn.
I couldn't deny her affection.

"But when"—Hodgkins cast a sheepish, half-defiant glare
at Nash—"but when I would return home from work after
having solved, or nearly solved, some particularly important
problem, Carolyn would be extremely affectionate. She—
she would sleep in my room that night."

Nash said nothing, waiting.

"As an illustration," Hodgkins continued after a moment,
"let me use that schematic drawing I spoke of before. While
I would be working my slow way through that drawing,
Carolyn would keep pace with me by holding my hand, by
kissing me warmly each evening as I came home. But on
the day I had mastered it, the day I had enmeshed the whole
and understood the scheme completely—on that day Carolyn would know what happened, would know that I had
solved another knotty problem and it was on its way to the
proper government agencies. That night then—that night
she would delight me, would live with me again the early
days of our marriage when I was a younger and more active
man. And before the next morning she would know what
had been accomplished. She would know each exact detail
and could, if need be, sit down and make a copy of that
drawing. All this without a spoken word passing my lips."

He used the soiled handkerchief to mop his face. "And
that, Mr. Nash, is my theory. I believe I know how mental

telepathy works and I believe I have unwillingly proved it."

Nash opened his eyes and shifted his position in the chair. He fastened his penetrating gaze upon Hodgkins. "If you were an archeologist instead of a telemetry expert, that form of telepathy wouldn't have startled you so. Astonished and pleased you—yes, but you would have probably recognized it."

"I would?"

"Yes. Making due allowance for the scanty information available today, there's reason to believe your telepathy was practiced among the Sumerians some five to seven thousand years ago. The art has since become lost."

"Is that a fact? Are you an archeologist?"

"The armchair variety," Nash said. "But you seem to have overlooked the most important point right now. What did your wife *do* with the knowledge she gained from you? What did she do with those government secrets? Pass them along to someone else perhaps?"

"I don't know. I have no idea. I never saw anything suspicious that would suggest such a thing. But then, I wouldn't see that, would I?"

"No, that too would be behind your back."

"Do you—do you think perhaps Carolyn ran away with a spy?"

"Don't be so melodramatic," Nash snapped. "Spies don't run away with anyone—they travel alone. No, she didn't run away with a spy."

Hodgkins melted back into his chair, dejected. "Do you understand the terrible trouble I'm in? I have my convictions and I believe utterly in them. But can I take them to the police? Would they believe me? Can I tell my troubles to the security agents who guard the plant out there? What would that psychiatrist say if I told him all that I have told you? What would happen to me? And think, man—do I want to turn my own beloved wife over to the law, assuming they would believe me?"

Nash shook his head. "Friend, you've got my sympathy. You're in a very clever trap, the damn'dest and most foolproof trap I've ever seen." He interlaced his fingers, staring at the scientist. "You were trapped into marriage, believe me. Baited and trapped by a beautiful woman because of what you were then. To add to your own misfortunes, you fell in love with her . . ." He paused, let his gaze drift slowly around the walls of the room and then back to the man. "Or maybe you were made to fall in love with her."

"I—don't think I understand."

"I'm not surprised. Few mortals do." Nash paused again, frowning. "You still haven't told me why you and Carolyn separated."

"Why—I was sent home from the plant! That silly psychiatrist prescribed rest. And I was of no use to Carolyn after I had left the Ridge."

Nash considered the answer. "That isn't all of it." He bounded from the chair and strode to the window.

"I don't know what you mean."

"I think you do. Which happened first, your being sent home, or your wife walking out?"

"They—they both happened on the same day. Carolyn left the same afternoon I came home."

"That's better, and that's quite interesting. We will assume that she deserted you when she discovered your usefulness was over. As you say, she could—siphon no more secrets from you if you no longer worked there. But that still isn't all. Before that afternoon, what caused your dismissal? Why were you in such a state that the psychiatrist told you to go home?"

"Carolyn."

"Carolyn? What did she do?"

"Nothing obvious. But for weeks she gave every indication of being finished with me. I gained the distinct impression that she was mentally packing up and preparing to leave. I worried about it. I didn't want to part with her. I suppose I worried myself into such a state that I visited the doctor. And he—you know the rest."

Nash put his forehead to the pane of window glass and looked down. "I know that your wife realized you were finished before you did. The point is, finished in what way? You still have your mental and physical health, you *still* had an excellent job, and that particular agency of the government doesn't send you to a glue factory when they are done with you. So how and why were you finished?"

"I can't imagine," Hodgkins answered evasively.

Nash stared at his own close reflection in the window glass. "Perhaps not—and perhaps you can. I want to think of that a moment. It's highly important that we discover *why* your wife decided you were finished, *why* she prepared to leave you." He fell silent for a moment musing. Traffic noise reached up, thin and diluted with distance. "What about your work on the Ridge? Had you just wound up some really important job?"

"Well—yes." Hodgkins grew uneasy.

"Don't worry—I'm not going to pump you."

"Official secrecy, you know," the man said pompously.

Nash turned slowly around to stare down at him, not attempting to conceal the scorn in his expression or his voice. "Hodgkins, I'm laughing at you now. Not at what you have told me up to this moment; I made a promise and I intend to keep it. But I'm laughing at what you've just said."

The expert returned his glance, puzzled and ill at ease.

Nash flicked a pointed finger. "Other than those people down there on the street who aren't able to think beyond the printed lines of a newspaper, there are only two kinds of men in all the world who still believe there are keepable secrets in modern science! One of those men is the blind, awkward and fumbling politician—and we can dismiss him because he suffers his occupational disease. The other man is a jealous researcher."

"But I—"

"But you have so narrowed your mind and your former capacity for intelligent reasoning that you now fall into the second category. You were even startled when I looked at that signboard stuck in your lapel and told you where you worked. Can you comprehend the iron grip that the secrecy fetish has on your mind? Realistic secrecy in modern science is a farce. What did you tell me awhile ago about borrowing books and magazines from the library to aid your studies? Do you think men all over the world have forgotten what was printed in them, that tens of thousands of scattered copies were gathered up and burned? Do you actually believe that only your group and your government know how to build weapons, control all the knowledge?" Nash stabbed out a finger to emphasize his point. "I feel sorry for you, Hodgkins, and all those others who think as you do. You have no secrets."

"Our security people—"

"The security people worship at the feet of the same idol and believe in the same religion; and in a half-dozen other countries a half-dozen other security forces worship similar idols. I'm laughing at you, Hodgkins, because all the idols are images of the same god, all the religions are one. All the security forces struggle to prevent the same 'secrets' leaking to the outer countries."

"I've heard the theory discussed," Hodgkins said.

"So? You think it an abstract matter? Listen then, friend, while I destroy your religion. Your government long ago invented and put to use an inverted-Y gun for detonating the atomic bomb. A dozen years ago, Russia developed an inverted-Y gun for detonating the atomic bomb. Less than six years ago, England examined and discarded the principle of an inverted-Y gun for detonating an atomic bomb. Secrecy—hell!"

Hodgkins looked his firm disbelief.

Nash's voice dropped softly. "A great and pompous to-do is made about the size of the critical mass necessary to detonate that bomb. The people making the greatest fuss are the most deluded." His voice dropped still lower, almost to a whisper. "Hodgkins—what would happen in this room, to this building, if I were able to bring together very quickly just twenty-two pounds of pure U-235? Twenty-two point seven pounds, to be exact?"

He waited for an answer but there was none. The scientist stared numbly at his hands lying limp in his lap.

"I didn't obtain that information by stealth or trickery," Nash declared. "And you can tell your security agents about me, if you like. When they come trooping in here I'll show them where it was published, chapter and verse." He moved away from the desk to pace the room. "I can also tell you the present size of the bomb casing, as opposed to that ungainly giant dropped on Hiroshima—surely you recall that it was necessary to gouge out the interior of a plane to house that one. And I know—if you don't—that an inglorious thing like a three-dollar alarm clock was the timing device in that first bomb. Today, they're using frequency impulses. Now will you believe me—there are no real secrets?"

"I can't—tell you anything. I have sworn."

"All right," Nash said in resignation, "keep your oath if it will help you keep your sanity. I'll tell you. You don't have to answer; you needn't say a word. I'll know by your face whether I'm right or wrong."

He went back to the window to place his forehead against the cool glass. Hodgkins glanced up briefly, stared at the back of his neck and dropped his eyes again.

"I think your wife left you for two reasons," Nash began. "And I think she knew you were finished in more ways than one. First and foremost, she knew you had finished the very important work you were doing on the Ridge. What could that work be? The major restrictions of the place were dropped in 1949 and now the public runs through the town as if it were a railroad station. Other plants in other places have seized the initiative and Oak Ridge could be compared to a ghost town; it played the star role years ago." The tall man turned his back to the window and settled his gaze on Hodgkins.

"Today, places like Hanford, and Brookhaven, and the Savannah River project are old hat—and Oak Ridge is *supposed* to be old hat. But actually it isn't—you are still working there, or were up until a few weeks ago, working on a highly important matter. Now, what is so important in telemetry these days to keep you at Ridge?"

Hodgkins did not look up.

"It might be a special reaction motor," Nash said softly, watching the half-averted face. "They are installing one in that ocean liner over on the east coast; and one of the electrical companies up north has been trying for years to build one into a plane." He paused again, waiting for the words to sink in. "It *might* be an atomic drive for a deep-space vehicle."

Hodgkins had moved. Nash watched him closely.

"It might be a heavy-duty reaction motor designed to fit into a special kind of ship with a special kind of problem to overcome." The man in the chair was visibly nervous, and Nash pushed on. "It *could* be a small-scale pile capable of developing a tremendous kick—something, say, which would drive a probe into deep space. And *that*, in turn, would require a whole new concept in telemetry mechanics."

Nash whirled to the window, suddenly satisfied with the results of his probing. That last shot had told.

"As a matter of fact," he continued calmly, "the NASA program for deep-space probes is well under way, despite the budget cutting, despite the accidents and the talk of a deliberate slow-down. I think those laboratories in California have delivered an atomic reaction motor to the Cape; I think the technicians at the Cape have fitted the motor into a ship. And I think now you have completed your work. I think you have sent to the Cape a whole new telemetric package to manage that ship, manage it at tremendous stellar distances." Nash crooked his head to look back at the seated man. "One of the trade journals has been discussing the Tau Ceti system. I think they let the cat from the bag."

The secrecy-conscious expert fidgeted in his chair but said nothing.

Nash said, "I think the California labs have invented a whole new drive system, a new power train. Perhaps a reaction motor using heavy water in some new but exciting way." (Hodgkins had jumped.) "Tau Ceti—imagine that! Will the ship carry men?"

"I—don't know," Hodgkins told him slowly.

"No, I suppose you don't. The idol must be worshiped at all costs." He lapsed into silence.

For long minutes there was no sound in the room but the curiously loud ticking of a watch somewhere in Hodgkins's clothing. Down the corridor an elevator door clanged.

"Uh—about Carolyn."

"Yes—we must still face the problem of your missing wife." Nash sighed and his body relaxed. "We can safely assume we know *one* of the reasons why she left you. Once she learned all there was to know about your latest work, learned the type of vessel for which it was designed, your usefulness to her was nearly over. Mind you I'm not saying that she couldn't have continued to live with you, couldn't have continued to pry out your trade secrets. She could have stayed. But she didn't. That is the most important, and I want to very much know why she didn't stay."

"I'm very glad you understand," Hodgkins said wearily. "I didn't know where else to turn."

Nash looked down on him curiously. "You want me to find her, I take it—to attempt a reconciliation?"

"Anything, Mr. Nash, just anything at all! I want to see Carolyn again, to touch her, to talk to her. I'm miserable without her and I want her to know it—if she will consent to see me again if only for a little while. I want her near me, I want to persuade her to come home."

"How do you know she is still in town?"

"I just think so—I sort of sense her presence. I saw her once, you know, just once about a week ago. She was entering a hotel. I ran after her but she was gone. The man at the desk threatened to have me arrested for creating a disturbance."

Nash pushed a pencil and paper across the desk to him. "Write down her description—make it complete. The date you last saw her, the clothes she was wearing, the clothes she took with her when she moved out. How much money did she have; did she have a separate bank account? Can she drive a car; does she have one? The names of her friends, if any. The name of the beauty shop she patronized, the stores where she usually bought her clothes. Did she have a checking or charge account? Put it all down—everything you think of."

Hodgkins held the pencil in a tight grasp, staring at Nash.

"What's the matter?" Nash asked.

"There is one thing about her description . . ."

"What?"

"Her eyes are yellow—like yours."

"Put it down," Nash replied. He studied the scientist closely as the man bent over the pencil.

There was still something here that hadn't come out. Still a vital and important something which lacked an answer.

Perhaps Hodgkins himself wasn't aware of it, couldn't tell it. He seemed alert enough within the bounds of his own profession (making due allowances for the crippling security fetish) but he was woefully ignorant in other matters. The woman (and a hidden confederate, perhaps?) had skillfully trapped him into marriage and then patiently waited several years for the jackpot to pay off. Three weeks ago it had apparently paid off. She traded on his gullibility and his lofty ambitions for the future; it wasn't too fantastic to assume the woman knew or had learned of those ambitions and wanted desperately to be with him when they bore fruit—that she might benefit personally from them.

She had abandoned him now, not after failure but on the threshold of his success. Why?

Not because of his emotional breakdown. She herself had caused that, had caused his growing anxiety long weeks before the breakdown and the dismissal. Had she not given him cause to suspect she was leaving, not demonstrated in some way that she was breaking up their marriage, he would not have been sent home from his job—thus cutting off her supply of information. She was the direct cause. But why? And that long thirst for information, the continual prying in a field far outside the usual woman's world—that was to be remarked. It revealed much of Carolyn Hodgkins. He didn't need the man's information that Carolyn Hodgkins had yellow eyes. It was her search for information that revealed her to him. The thirst, and the method of obtaining it. Nash had a brief moment of genuine pity for Hodgkins. His very early years of marriage, during their "closeness," must have been enjoyable in the extreme.

But there remained the enigmatic missing factor. Why had Carolyn Hodgkins coldly abandoned a first-class information carrier? And long before his usefulness was over, reasonably long before his latest work could be put to practical use? If he had finished that work some three weeks ago, the children of *Apollo* could not leap into space today or tomorrow.

Nash shook his head.

Hodgkins pushed the paper back across the desk. "I'm afraid that's the best I can do. It is strange how few details of a woman's dress you can remember—when you have to."

"Good enough." Nash studied the neat handwriting. "Did your wife have any hobbies? Collect anything—stamps, coins, anything? Bric-a-brac, maybe?"

"No, not that I recall. Oh, she did have a bull." Hodgkins closed his eyes, picturing it.

"Bull?"

"A toy of some sort, I think. Stood about six inches high; I thought it was a china bull but it was made of some unbreakable material. She kept it in her bedroom. Do you mean to tell me you can make deductions from that?"

Nash shrugged. "You never know. People don't abandon hobbies and habits when they change their lives. I wonder if I could drop out to the house some evening . . . ? Look around, get the feel of the place? I might be able to find something you'd never think of."

"Why—certainly. I'd be pleased to have you. You can find my number in the phone book."

"Will do—soon. I'd like to talk to you in your own home; maybe the familiar surroundings will help to relieve your nervousness. And I may have something to report."

"I've never done this sort of thing before, you know. My doctor—you seemed to be the only one I could confide in. I'm very glad you didn't laugh at me." A shadow crossed his face and he abruptly arose from the chair, shifting the straw hat from hand to hand. "Is there anything else, Mr. Nash?"

"No." Gilbert Nash put out his hand and clasped that of his visitor. A jolt ran through him. "Leave the rest to me. If she can be found, I'll find her; if she can be persuaded to see you, I'll arrange a meeting in some neutral place. If she refuses to see you, I'll find out why and deliver the message." He struggled to keep his face an emotionless mask as he held the contact. "I can't promise you what kind of results I'll get, but it will be something—something definite. And in the meantime I'm going to give you much the same advise that psychiatrist gave—but with a difference. Don't stay home and mope. Go out and get drunk. Try to enjoy yourself for once in your life."

He broke off the long handclasp, and the unhappy man was gone—moving slowly toward the door, peeping cautiously into the corridor before entering it, softly closing the door behind him and ambling away. Nash could follow his hesitant steps toward the elevator. After a space the elevator door opened and closed, and the machine descended to street level.

Nash stared down at his open palm.

He knew with deadly certainty why Hodgkins's wife had deserted him. It had been a numbing jolt.

Chapter 4

DIKTY APPROACHED his base of operations and his morning routine with a cold pipe and still colder thoughts. He felt old and washed out. The morning was already cloudy and damp with promise of rain to come, and that served only to increase his irritation. His breakfast had been tasteless on his tongue, gulped down automatically and without appreciation, while innumerable cups of too-hot coffee had failed to wash away the weariness within him. And his wife— He couldn't remember when it had been necessary to apologize to his wife before, but he had done so this morning, halfway through the meal. He hadn't realized he was talking so roughly, so thoughtlessly. And he might as well admit it—he was getting old for the job; he could no longer stay up all night and still feel human the next day. This was a job for younger men.

His was a second-floor office, consisting of two plain rooms tucked away at the back of the corridor. The solid, metal-sheathed door opening into the first room bore only a number, nothing else.

Shirley Hoffman waited behind her typewriter, doing nothing. She looked up brightly as he came in.

"Good morning, Mr. Dikty."

"Don't be so damned cheerful," he retorted. "I'm not in the mood."

Hoffman regarded him owlishly. "Little woman been beating you again?"

Dikty stopped, "I'm sorry. I was short tempered with my wife too, and that shouldn't happen. Business is on the bad side this morning. I don't like unpleasantness and I don't like night work; these last seven or eight hours have given me a bellyful of both." He removed the raincoat from across his arm and hung it up. "Lock the door and come in."

Hoffman moved from behind her desk. "The telephone operator tells me that Washington has been calling. They will call again at nine thirty." She snapped the lock on the metal-covered door.

Dikty glanced at his watch and absently studied the phone. "Cummings has my telegram, apparently. He doesn't like it either." He stalked across the room into the inner office, the girl trailing after him. Dikty seated himself and stared moodily through the window at the dullish sky, while the secretary poised her pencil over pad and waited.

"Hoffman," he said tiredly to the window and the sky beyond, "when you grow up, marry a dull and stolid man and have a happy life. Marry a painter or a plumber or a projectionist, I don't care. But don't be a career girl and above all, a career girl in our dirty racket!"

"Thank you, Mr. Dix."

He moved slowly around to face her, scowling. "All right, do as you damned please! But I'm the kind of a man who says, I told you so."

"Rough, I gather?"

"Rough." Dikty nodded and absently pulled his pipe from his pocket. "Rougher than hell on an old man like me." He discovered the pipe in his hands, filled it and lit up. "This is for Cummings," he said after a moment. "It concerns an

Oak Ridge man plus the subject under previous discussion."
He pointed the pipestem at her notebook.

"Gregg Hodgkins, age forty-six, married, owning a home
at 2334 North Shasta Drive. No children, no near relatives.
Now— Until three weeks ago, Hodgkins was a competent
and dependable technician employed on a special and hurry-
up project at Oak Ridge." Dikty paused to collect a memory. "Hodgkins was working on Code four-four-seven,
sharing co-responsibility for leadership on same. For some
six or seven weeks prior to the particular date three weeks
ago, Hodgkins exhibited growing signs of nervousness, mental fatigue and possible instability. This was noted, but beyond a constant watch nothing was done about it, due to
the fact the Code four-four-seven was rapidly nearing
completion ahead of schedule and the stress was attributed
to that. In addition, his co-leader and several of his fellow
workers on the project all exhibited similar nervousness,
leading the plant authorities to believe that all concerned
were sharing the same anxiety over the coming ultimate
success or failure of the experiment.

"Code four-four-seven was completed successfully and all
men concerned with the thing reverted back to their normal
selves with varying degrees of rapidity, except Hodgkins. He
was then moved to a separate and harmless project and
placed under continuous observation, but before plant authorities could do more he took matters into his own hands.

"He first visited his family doctor, Charles Barrett, 260
Weinburg Building. He told the doctor that he was ex-
periencing domestic difficulties which had become rather
acute in recent weeks and attempted to fix the blame for said
difficulties on his wife. He further stated that his wife was—
or had recently become—more intelligent than he, and
that this matter embittered him. The doctor assured him
that he was a healthy man, physically, and sent him to the
plant psychiatrist."

Dikty lifted the pipe to his mouth, discovered that the glow had died, and applied a second match.

"Montgomery, the psychiatrist, reports a similar story. Hodgkins visited him, told him of his difficulties at home and repeated the belief that his wife now outranked him in intelligence quotient. Hodgkins gave a long and involved recital of his aims, hopes, and beliefs, chief among which was that as a young man he had wanted a smart and intelligent mate to help him reach his goals, that he had deliberately and with careful study chosen this particular woman as being suitable to his purposes—or ideals. In recent years, however, he had become dissatisfied with their marriage because, as he put it, she apparently continued to gain intelligence at a rate exceeding his. This condition eventually unnerved him, coupled to the strain connected with Code four-four-seven.

"Pending further investigation of the case, the psychiatrist sent him home and thereafter made periodic calls at the house to check up. Hodgkins's mental condition became worse for reasons mentioned next below.

"His wife deserted him on the same day that he was sent home. Actual reasons for separation not apparent to me, beyond those statements mentioned above. After two weeks of continued study, the psychiatrist prepared a recommendation that Hodgkins be permanently dismissed from government service—although that recommendation was not made known to him. In addition, the usual shadow would be assigned to him to determine if he could hold his silence.

"Meanwhile, the wife moved into the May Hotel here; but moved out again several days later when she discovered that he had followed her and created a scene at the desk. The wife's present location is unknown to me. She left no forwarding address and no discernible trail. I am of course, concentrating on that angle in an attempt to locate her. Nothing more happened until yesterday.

"Early yesterday morning, Hodgkins left his home in a state of visible agitation and after wandering about the streets for many hours, called upon our subject—the subject under previous discussion and investigation. I am totally unable to discover what went on between them. The shadow reports that Hodgkins was closeted with subject for more than an hour, but that he could determine nothing of the conversation they held. In regards this failure, I decided to wire the subject's office for sound and have taken steps to plant several microphones there. I regret that I did not do so earlier.

"As to Hodgkins's visit to the subject, I am unable to decide which of two reasons is the probable one. Fresh in mind is the McKeown case of some time back; Hodgkins may have decided to sell his information, but if this be true, how he became acquainted with our subject and what led him to believe the subject was interested in buying, I do not know. As mentioned in previous conversations, I have no knowledge or suspicion that subject is purchasing information.

"Unofficially, I am inclined to think that Hodgkins visited the subject for a second and rather obvious reason. Considering the subject's advertised profession, Hodgkins's recent separation from his wife and subsequent failure to meet her again, only one fact prevents me from leaping to that rather obvious conclusion. The fact that the man is under our investigation, and that the coincidences involved are far too numerous and too startling. Are we to assume that this is but another one?"

Dikty turned slightly in his chair to waggle the pipe-stem at the girl. "And Hoffman, if you haven't discovered by this time the identity of the subject we are discussing, you may as well kiss your career good-bye." He studied her for a brief moment, the lines of weariness standing out on his face. "On the other hand, if you admit to being nosey and mention his name aloud, you can also kiss it good-bye." He gave her a tired smile. "Now, do you want to marry the plumber?"

The girl returned the smile with spirit. "Not just yet. I don't plan to marry early."

"That's what I said, a long time ago. I met her at a square dance. And this morning I had to apologize to her for the first time in my life." His eyes went back to the window and the threatening sky. "Well, suit yourself. You and I and the rest of us are involved in a game that is alternately boring and deadly. You'll have to make your own decision. Let's get back . . .

"After leaving the subject's office in an apparently calmer state of mind, Hodgkins again wandered aimlessly through the streets for several hours and finally entered a secondhand shop where he attempted to purchase a revolver. The proprietor refused to sell him a weapon at that time, explaining that first he must obtain a police permit to carry a weapon. Hodgkins told the proprietor he would obtain one, and picked out a gun, asking the proprietor to lay it aside until he returned. The proprietor did so. Hodgkins then left the shop and did not return.

"He next visited a sporting goods store and again attempted to buy a revolver, again being told that first a permit was necessary before they could sell him the weapon. Hodgkins repeated the earlier procedure of choosing a gun and the store clerk set it aside for him. The shadow reports that both shopkeepers were in no way suspicious and that Hodgkins exhibited a calm, friendly manner at all times. (These men have learned to judge to some degree the type of person wanting hand weapons.) After these two attempts, Hodgkins purchased one copy of each of several newspapers available at a corner stand and retired to a small restaurant. He read them all thoroughly. The shadow states that it was quite apparent Hodgkins was searching for some particular item.

"He finally discarded the papers and took a taxi to his home, remaining there the rest of the day and evening." Dikty paused to examine the ash in his pipe. "And I wish I could do the same."

Hoffman glanced up at him with a shy speculative expression. She rolled the pencil between her fingers.

"Go on," Dikty invited, "say it."

"I would judge," she answered slowly, "that Hodgkins visited subject and retained his services. To find the missing wife. I would further judge that Hodgkins intended to shoot his wife—when they again met."

"Correct."

A roll of heavy thunder followed his agreement.

"And that he lost his nerve when he discovered the red tape necessary to buy a gun . . ." She paused to frown. "No, not quite that. He didn't lose his nerve, he merely realized a gun would have to be obtained in another way."

"Nearly correct," Dikty nodded. "He may also have realized that a gun wasn't necessary at all. He's a smart chap, remember that. You or I could name a dozen seemingly innocent things to put in her coffee, but then he was no longer in a position to feed her anything. It may be that he searched for some other means of reaching her over a distance." He went back to searching the dull sky. "I wish I knew what it was he was looking for in the papers."

"The personal advertisements— No, he read them quite thoroughly, didn't he?"

"He did. He was searching for news of some nature."

"Something the subject planted in his mind?"

Dikty made as if to answer and then paused. "Yes," he said after a moment. "It could be."

The telephone rang. He consulted his watch. Hoffman answered the instrument, nodded, and handed it to him.

"Dikty, here." A pause. "Yes, he did. Shortly after midnight last night. No, no not yet. They are searching." Another and longer pause. "I am, constantly. Subject has made no move. The occurrence hasn't yet appeared in the local papers. It will tonight." Another pause. "Oak Ridge will issue the explanation. Yes, probably. You what . . . ?" There was a long period of silence in the office. "I'm making out a detailed report now. It will be in your hands in the morning. Hodgkins and our subject made personal contact, rather suddenly. Sought him out, yes. Yes, I think that too. All right." One final pause. "I will." And he hung up.

Hoffman waited expectantly.

Dikty regarded the cradled phone rather somberly, moved his eyes to the darkened sky beyond the window for a reflective moment and then swung back to the girl. "The new operative is on the job, but hasn't yet reported in. Apparently he still doesn't know what happened last night." He pointed to the notebook with a stained pipestem.

"At ten minutes past twelve last night, a neighbor at 2336 North Shasta Drive telephoned the police, reporting that she had heard a noise next door resembling a gunshot. The police arrived at twelve sixteen to find the house dark and locked; after some wasted minutes they gained entrance by forcing the kitchen door. Hodgkins was discovered dead in his wife's bedroom, stretched across the bed.

"The man was shot through the head from front to back, the gun being placed in the open mouth and fired. It was a .32 caliber Smith and Wesson and was found on the floor near the body. The weapon was well oiled and of course contained no prints whatsoever. Police immediately made skin tests of deceased's fingers and found slight traces of oil but none of burned powder."

"Dead," the girl said in a small voice.

"Very dead," Dikty agreed. "Through the mouth. We will have to await a criminologist's report on that, but I've heard that sailors and women frequently select such a method in suicide. Messy. You should have seen the bed."

"No, thanks." Hoffman repressed a shudder. "What does that last mean? Oil and powder stains?"

"A well-oiled gun will not retain fingerprints, fiction to the contrary. Oil stains on Hodgkins's fingers indicate he handled the weapon, but the lack of powder stains indicates he did not fire it. Again, we'll have to await an expert's opinion; but it's out of my field. I believe they have some sort of iodine vapor treatment to develop hidden stains and prints and so forth. Well—here's the rest of it.

"Police searched the house and found oil spots on certain items of Hodgkins's clean clothing in a drawer, leading them at first to believe he had hidden the gun there. In the light of subsequent disclosures mentioned above, they now believe he did not possess a gun and was murdered by the assailant's weapon. Assailant of course did not know that Hodgkins had twice attempted and failed to purchase a gun earlier that day; therefore the planting of oil spots and leaving the gun on the scene to suggest suicide was patently false.

"Meanwhile, the assigned shadow (or his relief), waiting in a car nearby, was of course on duty and reported that no one entered or left the house to the best of his knowledge. He heard the shot but decided against entering for fear the police would discover him there, and because his routing instructions did not cover such emergency action. Oak Ridge has not seen fit to notify the police that the shadow was nearby or even to reveal his existence, or the reason he was trailing the deceased, believing that it can add nothing to the case.

"Police of course are seeking Hodgkins's widow for information. So am I. I'm attending the funeral tomorrow to see who might turn up. End of report."

Outside the rain began to come down. Dikty glowered at it. Shirley followed his glance to the window and watched the rain for long minutes before asking, "The widow?"

"Not in my book."

"But definitely not suicide?"

"No."

She said, "I wonder . . . ?"

"Police action in a murder case," Dikty explained, "is first to establish method and motive, I believe. The method was quite plain, quite messy. The motive frequently leads them to the murderer." He searched through the rain, seeking the outlines of a building down the street.

"I can read the thoughts on your face," Shirley said to him.

"Can you now? Do you also see his name there?"

"You told me never to mention his name aloud."

Chapter 5

GILBERT NASH WAITED motionless in the rainswept darkness, a tall and lonely figure unseen and unsuspected in the
drenched night. His eyes were focused on the house. Most
of the neighboring homes were darkened, their occupants
long since retired, while only here and there an occasional
window continued to spill light. The houses on either side
of the Hodgkins domicile were black and silent; the neigh-
borhood's brief moment of excitement and scandal was
done. No automobiles moved on the rainy street.

Still Nash waited, his eyes watching for movement and
his thoughts turned inward upon Hodgkins and the place
he had called home up until twenty-four hours ago. Hodgkins had left home. He had briefly seen the man again that
afternoon, seen the remains; the mortician had worked
minor miracles on a face which had been troubled, on a
skull which only half existed. Hodgkins's face, ridden with
uncertainty and gnawing fear, a face that hadn't known true
peace for many years—until shortly after midnight last night.
The bewildered man and his dreams, his many plans for the
future, his discoveries—including the one in the library who
had soon become his wife.

There were many things an eulogist might say on behalf

of Gregg Hodgkins, but two of his outstanding discoveries had small chance of being mentioned at a funeral oration or listed in his obituary. Both accomplishments lay in his chosen field: communications.

Hodgkins had helped to build the means of managing a starship on the incredibly long flight to Tau Ceti, or beyond; had helped to fashion an electronic system which was capable of guiding that ship, listening to it, taking its pulse, manipulating its minute-by-minute workings, controlling its experiments, reading the results of the experiments, approving or rejecting them, maintaining two-way communication between ship and base, directing its course through the Tau Ceti system, and then bringing it home again. His work in telemetry—along with the labor of his colleagues—was expected to do all that without error or mishap and without on-board human guidance. Hodgkins deserved at least a small monument for that feat, but he wouldn't get it. He would likely get no public recognition at all.

Nash carefully shifted his position, easing back out of the rain. The remaining windows were going dark. He listened to the night and watched the street.

Gregg Hodgkins had made another startling discovery in communications, but his obituary wouldn't mention it.

Hodgkins the husband, as opposed to the scientist, had rediscovered a long lost property in communications although he didn't fully appreciate it as such; with his wife's assistance he had revived a lost art almost as old as humanity itself. While the Rhine and allied experimenters played with cards and continued their investigations into telepathy over a distance, or through barriers, with varying haphazard results, Gregg Hodgkins had stumbled and fallen over the one true application of thought transference and revived it for a brief moment in history. It disconcerted him.

Not being a Methuselah, he couldn't know that his unorthodox method of transference had flourished briefly in

earth's prehistoric past, that it had been practiced as long
ago as the Akkad Dynasty some seven thousand years before his birth. He had no knowledge that the "mental telepathy" occurring between his wife and himself was a part of
the everyday lives of the ancient Sumerians, that it had
enabled the legendary Gilgamesh to overcome his only
mortal enemy, and that it had become lost the *first* time at
the end of that age. He couldn't know that the strange art
had reappeared only briefly during the Third Dynasty of
Ur and then vanished again for thousands of years—until
he married Carolyn. Hodgkins would be hard put to explain it if he had known it.

His wife might have explained it, if she had felt anything
other than contempt for him; Nash might have explained
it, if he'd thought it wise; but present-day scholars of the
conservative school would have nothing but derisive laughter for the notion that the ancients sometimes practiced
"mental telepathy" by a touch, a kiss, or a coupling—and the
more liberal scholars would have difficulty in hiding an
amused grin. Gregg Hodgkins's two discoveries would go
unknown, unmarked, and a fine old Sumerian art would
remain lost.

The obituary would prattle only of the commonplace,
the small gravestone would remain blank but for name and
appropriate dates.

Nash left his protected position and advanced on the
house. The police had boarded up the broken window in
the kitchen door with a thin sheet of plywood, had locked
the door again and taken the key with them. Nash moved
softly across the tiny porch and put his weight to the door.
It was solid and unyielding. He placed his hands against
one corner of the plywood and pressed in, gently easing the
nails free of their grip. When a small space had been opened
he reached through and turned the knob from the inside.

The door opened to him. He stepped silently into the dark kitchen and closed the door behind him, pushing the plywood back into place. The house smelled of stale cigars, of musty unclean odors.

Nash waited there for a long moment, probing the blackened silence of the dead house, imagining that he could almost feel the past presence of the scientist. Hodgkins's personality still clung to the darkened interior, clashing somehow with the stale smoke of the recent intruders. There was nothing to suggest a similar presence for the wife. Her subtle, feminine aura had departed with her some three weeks before, had swept through the door with her and away like a live, obedient thing. There was not now a wisp to indicate she had ever been there. Nash wondered about her briefly, wondered if she had ever really *lived* in the house despite the number of years she stayed there? Or had she been akin to the overnight traveler who does not live but exists in his hotel room?

He wondered too if she had known the eerie, haunting shock he'd felt, when he shook hands with her husband? Had that shock struck her suddenly as it had hit him, or had it grown with a quiet intensity over a period of months, causing her to become slowly aware of impending events? That one final handclasp had told him quite clearly why Carolyn Hodgkins deserted her husband. She was about to become a widow. And for some reason she did not care to be at home when the state of widowhood arrived.

Nash moved out of the kitchen to explore the house, shielding the flashlight's beam with his hand.

First a bathroom and then a bedroom met his inquiring eyes—Hodgkins's bedroom, as he determined after a few minutes examination. The man's clothing still hung in the closet, carelessly rumpled. A few books on the bedside table, a rundown alarm clock, a layer of dust. The dresser drawers had been left hanging open after the visit of the police, and

Nash abandoned any hope of finding the clothing containing the oil spots. He peered into the top drawer to discover a few handkerchiefs, a couple of pairs of socks, a neatly folded woolen scarf, a used but unbroken shoestring and a chewed pencil. To judge by the marks in the dust, a large picture had been removed from the dresser top—Carolyn's picture, undoubtedly, taken along by the police to aid them in their search for the woman.

Traces of white powder clung to every surface; the police never bothered to clean up their fingerprinting paraphernalia. Nash slipped his hands into his pockets and gave the room a last glance.

He walked through the adjoining bath into another room, quite evidently her bedroom. The bed had been shoved back out of the way, perhaps to clear a space so that the police photographer might completely cover the interior. The mattress was bare, the bedclothing gone—to the police station, the laundry or the incinerator. Nash paused beside the bed to examine the mattress and the dull bloodstain, to judge how the body had sprawled across it. He failed to draw a clear-cut logical image. Hodgkins would probably have been standing beside the bed if he was murdered; lying on it if he killed himself. The blood stain gave no hint.

Nash retreated to the bathroom and glanced again at the bed in Hodgkins's room. It was clean, dusty, unmussed. The man had been sleeping in his wife's bed during the three weeks following her departure. A curiously inverted form of revenge, or wishful thinking? Following a sudden thought, he bent down to investigate the catch on her bedroom door. The key still stood in the lock on her side of the panel. Keep out—no trespassing. Unless of course Hodgkins arrived home from work with new knowledge, new developments. Come in—welcome.

Carolyn was a bitch.

He moved around the bedroom, looking for traces of the

departed woman, peering at the dust along the window sills and under the bed. Hodgkins had been no tidy housekeeper. The vanity drawers were empty of everything but a fine layer of dust and a few overlooked hairpins. He picked up one of those, held it close to the beam of the tiny flashlight he carried. It imparted nothing but he dropped it into his pocket. There was a small empty bottle that had contained nail polish but now it was covered by the white powder. Nash did not touch it. The room contained nothing more of Carolyn Hodgkins, but he remained there in the darkness for many minutes searching for an impression, for an indefinable something that might suggest she had once dwelt there. Still nothing.

For a third time he stepped into the bathroom and flashed his light around, peering into the medicine cabinet above the sink, sighed his disappointment and at last walked through the other rooms of the house, rooms that had no real interest to him. They were comfortable by modern standards, well-to-do as fitted their late owner's station in life. No more. No touch of Carolyn Hodgkins.

Nash seated himself in one of the overstuffed chairs beside a cold fireplace, laced his fingers together beneath his chin and contemplated the empty darkness. The steady fall of rain was the only sound.

He thought he understood Hodgkins's wanting to sleep in his wife's bed after she had gone; the man was very human, no cold-blooded scientific monster manufacturing death in underground retreats, no sinister Hollywood ogre. And he partially understood Hodgkins's love for his wife— only partially. He still couldn't decide to his own satisfaction if that love affair had been genuine, or had been carefully planted in the man. It must certainly be hell to be *human* and not know your own mind—not know beyond all reasonable doubt. Not know if an emotion was your own, or a clever counterfeit implanted in you. But whatever it had been, it was real enough to the husband. He had fallen hopelessly in love with the woman that long ago night in a public library, and had continued to love her hopelessly until the hour and minute of his death.

Why had he wanted a gun?

To kill Carolyn? Quite possible. Men desperately in love sometimes did that when the objects of their affections deliberately held themselves aloof. To kill himself? Again, quite possible. Men desperately in love also sometimes resorted to that when frustrated.

And Carolyn Hodgkins had known she was about to become a widow. She had discovered that startling and disastrous fact on one of those erotic nights when her husband was permitted to share her bedroom. Rude, shattering discovery! Almost obscene, considering the time and place. Like inviting a coming corpse to share your bed. But why had he wanted a gun? To kill someone else? Hardly possible. Who else would be a likely candidate in Hodgkins's small circle of friends and business acquaintances? He had begun his search for a gun the same morning he had instigated a search for his wife. *Quick thought:* had the scientist intended to kill Nash? For what possible reason? Because he and the missing wife had eyes of a similar color? Suspicions aroused?

Consider that.

The drumming rain beat against the side of the house.

Hodgkins hadn't been deranged—the doctor and the plant psychiatrist would have known that. But the man had been bathed in misery and despair; he may have intended killing any one of the three of them—or more than one. Wife, investigator, himself, which? Still, there always remained the possibility he hadn't intended to shoot anyone, except in self-defense. He may have sought the gun for protection —against something unknown. *Was* there still a third party forming a triangle to the Hodgkins marriage?

Carolyn Hodgkins had known what was about to happen and had deserted the husband before she could become entangled in it. And *he* himself had discovered the approaching death when he shook hands with Hodgkins in the office. A man's future, like his present, like his past, is written on his mind and waiting to be read or lived. Hodgkins had no future. His wife had discovered that and vanished. She had known for some months that her husband was nearing the end of his life; she had been making preparations to leave him long weeks before she actually did, and those preparations were readily apparent to the man, forcing a crisis upon him. Even *he*, a stranger, had foreseen the shortness of Hodgkins's future, the nearby blank ending of the conscious mind during that brief handclasp as the scientist left the office.

But was there a third party lurking somewhere close?

He stiffened in the chair, chopping off his thoughts, as the minute sound carried him from the kitchen door.

There was a gentle forcing of the plywood such as he had done, and a moment later the knob turned to let the door swing quietly inward. The intruder paused a moment in the kitchen, again as he had done, to smell the stale air and probe the darkness of the house. He wondered if his own presence could be sensed. Again a tiny sound as the door was closed and then soft, cautious footsteps creeping across the kitchen floor. The footsteps hesitated in the blackness of the place and finally a small light flashed out, picking out the bedroom door in bold relief. The wife's bedroom.

Nash relaxed in the chair with a self-satisfied grin and let the footsteps go their way.

The newcomer poked about the bedroom in a rather noisy manner, opening drawers and peering behind things, moving the chair and bedside table, flashing the light around carelessly. The sounds came to a full and breathless stop twice. Once the prowler paused beside the bed and caught sight of the bloodstain, and again at the door leading to the bath and opposite bedroom. Nash listened intently. There was the low, secretive rattle of the key being withdrawn from the lock, and then the snap of purse clasps. The intruder then continued on into Hodgkins's bedroom and repeated the search only to emerge into the living room after a long and thoughtful interval. The pleasant odor of her perfume arrived with her.

Nash unlaced his fingers from beneath his chin but didn't stir in the comfortable chair. Before she could see him and be unduly frightened, he spoke quietly.

"Hello."

Her gasp was almost a scream, half smothered and quickly choked off as she remembered where she was. Again her light stabbed out, spotlighting him in the chair.

"Better put that out," he advised her. "Neighbors might see it."

The light stayed on him a moment or two longer and blinked off. He could not see her at all in the new blackness, and knew that she could see him but dimly.

"What are you doing here?" she demanded in fright.

"Meditating."

She had no ready answer.

"There isn't much to be found," he continued in a conversational tone, striving to put her at ease. "I imagine the police have removed most of it."

She sucked in her breath and started again. "I want to know what you are doing here!" The voice was small and strained, still frightened at discovering him.

"Don't you believe that I would come here to meditate? The house was fairly quiet, until you came barging in. You aren't very accomplished at housebreaking, you know—much too noisy." He listened to her rapid breathing in the darkness. "Oh, all right, I'm here for the same reason you are. Loot."

"I'm not looting!" she shot back.

"Searching then."

"Searching for what?" she demanded instantly.

"Anything," he told her calmly. "Anything at all that may prove useful."

"Useful? To whom?"

"To myself."

She hesitated. "What is your interest in . . . ?"

"Come now, let's not be naive as well as noisy."

She said nothing to that, standing across the room and peering at him. Nash locked his fingers in his lap, his eyes becoming used to the darkness again and pinpointing her. She remained only a dim figure against the far wall. "I notice," he said casually, "that you haven't asked my name, who I am. You must know me."

"I've seen you," was the grudging admission.

"How nice." He smiled. "And may I see you?"

"No! Don't move!"

"But why not? I'm quite sure you are an attractive woman; you have an attractive voice, and I like the perfume."

"Never mind that." A measure of self-control was returning to her voice.

"But I do mind that. I'm fond of women."

"I still want to know what you are doing here!"

"But I've already told you the truth, believe me. I was searching the place, as you have."

"In that chair?" she asked derisively.

"I had come to the end of my search—as empty-handed as you. And so I sat down to meditate."

"What were you meditating?"

He laughed. "I'm sorry, dear mysterious girl. My thoughts are my own, free and untaxed. You are the most inquisitive person I've met in a long time. Please tell me who you are?"

"No."

"Very well. I'll find out for myself."

There was a catch to her breath. "How . . . ?"

"I'll remember your voice, your perfume," he said chidingly. "I'll remember the way you walk. But I shall always remember your voice, even when it has lost its overtones of fright." He laughed again. "I'd like to become better acquainted with the voice. Oh, I'll find you."

"And then?" she asked.

He smiled to himself in the darkness; she really wanted to hear the answer. "It depends on the time, and the place. I may buy you a drink or a dinner, may ask you to dance or come and see my butterfly collection. Or I may ask you to remove your hat because you're obstructing the picture. We'll meet," he promised.

"Did—" She paused to rephrase the question. "Didn't you find anything? There is nothing in the house?"

"I found a hairpin," he acknowledged. "I have it here in my pocket. If you'd like one there are more in the vanity drawer."

She was obviously astonished. "What in the world do you want with a hairpin?"

"Oh—keep it. Perhaps try to match it to those you wear in your hair when I find you again, perhaps put it away as a sentimental bit of nothing. I don't know." He peered at her dim figure, wishing he could see her face more clearly. "I may even twist it out of shape—say fashion it into the horns of a bull, hold it over a flame." He was suddenly tense, awaiting her reaction.

The room was enveloped in silence with the two people regarding one another as duelists, each struggling to see the other better in the almost nonexistent light. The rain was a background of continual sound to their duel.

Her question was a taut whisper. *"Who are you?"*

"Not at all what I seem," he answered cheerfully, now suddenly relaxed. "And if I may suggest, much like you in that respect."

"But who are you?" she repeated insistently.

"Gilbert Nash," Gilbert Nash said. "Hours from nine until four." He glanced around the darkened room. "Special hours of meditation by appointment."

"Stop being silly. You know what I mean!"

Nash shrugged, forgetting she could not see him. "You wouldn't tell me your name. So . . ."

She said slowly, "I could make you tell."

He peered at her, amused. "I doubt it."

"Hodgkins visited you, didn't he? In your office?"

"Yes, he did. And don't bother asking the next question because I won't tell you the answer."

Again she said, slowly and suggestively, "I could make you tell me."

Nash dryly repeated his doubt, and added as an afterthought, "I'm not like Hodgkins."

There was a tight moment of silence before she continued. "I wasn't thinking of using force."

"I know very well what you were thinking," Nash told her, striving to conceal the sudden amusement in his voice. "And again, I say, I'm not Hodgkins."

"You seem so damned sure of yourself!"

"And you," he countered, "like so many women, seem to believe that one thing will open all doors."

"I think I could *hate* you."

"It's only a surface thought, dear girl. It'll melt away with time; I'm really a lovable character. You can't afford to hate me—not in your present position. But go home and have a good cry if it will help." He sat up in the chair and stretched. "I suggest we both go home—we've been here far too long. The neighbors may have seen your light or a prowl car may stop by on a routine check. Neither of us wants to be found here." He made as if to rise.

"Don't move," she warned quickly.

"All right," he agreed, "not until after you leave. But please start leaving, will you. I've lived too long to want to be shot now." He put out a hand. "Shake hands before you go—bosom buddies and all that?"

"*No!*"

She slowly edged along the wall, inching her way toward the kitchen door. Nash remained seated, following her cautious movements with a speculative gleam. The girl backed up to the door and fumbled with the doorknob; it swung open but she hesitated a moment, one hand on the knob.

"I'll find you," Nash called after her.

She was gone, leaving the door hanging open.

Nash left his chair and leaped across the silent room, dropping to one knee and focusing his light on the spot where she had stood for so long. A trace of dampness, of mud, but no clear impression. He moved on into the kitchen and knelt again at the door, studying the frightened woman's muddy prints on the linoleum. They were blurred and indistinct, much like his own nearby. He extinguished the light to stare through the open doorway at the rain.

"That certainly wasn't Carolyn Hodgkins," he said with satisfaction.

Gregg Hodgkins's funeral the following afternoon was a small, poorly attended affair for a man who had accomplished so much, for a man who had helped hurl a starship into space. The stonecutter still was censored.

Clustered together in a corner of the mortuary parlor were a knot of men who had known him and worked with him at Oak Ridge; his co-leader on the recent project, a group of others who had contributed their bit, the psychiatrist, and

perhaps one or two others from the front office who attended because they felt it their duty—not because they had
known the deceased. Scarcely a dozen in all. So much for
fame, for a genuine contribution to human progress.

There was still another man who sat apart and continually
glanced at his watch—Hodgkins's doctor, Nash guessed. And
there were two men who kept themselves carefully separated from each other. These two men constantly eyed
every other person in the room, speculating, weighing,
examining. Independently they swung around to stare at
Nash as he walked in. They might as well have worn blue
uniforms.

There was one other person in the room—a young woman.
She sat quietly still, listening to the sermon.

Nash deliberately seated himself near her, choosing a
chair slightly behind hers that he might study her much the
same as the two policemen were now studying him. She did
not match the description of Carolyn Hodgkins that the
husband had furnished, certainly did not appear to be the
forty-one that Carolyn was by "agreement" nor was she
someone who would pass as ten years younger—someone
who hadn't grown much older "than the day they were
married." This woman had not yet reached thirty. The hair
was of a different color, the height was not the same, nor the
approximate weight. He could not see her face clearly, and
had not seen the eyes at all; she hadn't turned when he sat
down behind her. She *was* aware of him. He knew that by
the sudden rigidity of her body, by the way she held her
head and kept her attention on the minister. But this was
not Carolyn Hodgkins.

Who then? What other woman had an interest in Gregg
Hodgkins, living or dead?

Near the end of the sermon, Nash both felt and heard
someone else come into the room. Someone took a chair
near the door. It seemed to be a man, judging by the

heaviness with which he seated himself, and after a few moments Nash copied the plain-clothes men by turning to look.

The government man, Dikty, was staring at him.

Nash gave him the briefest of nods, which was as briefly returned, and then both of them returned their attention to the funeral proceedings. Nash contented himself by staring at the back of the girl's neck, waiting for the long sermon to come to an end.

Afterward he stood outside the mortuary, waiting in the half-cloudy sunshine for the girl to pass by. A group of silent Oak Ridge men came out and moved down the sidewalk. Then the two plain-clothes men emerged from the door, fixed him with twin stares, and purposely approached him. He instantly guessed that Dikty had sent them. Dikty himself appeared in the door after a few moments and stayed there, pretending not to notice him or the policemen.

"Nash?" one of the men asked.

"Yes."

"We sort of wondered why you came down?"

"Hodgkins? Well—he was my client, for a time."

"How long a time?"

"Something like ten or twelve hours." Nash studied their faces seeking a hint as to their intentions.

"What did he want with you?"

"Asked me to locate his wife."

"That all?" the policeman asked suspiciously.

"That's all."

"It wasn't nothing to do with his job?"

"Absolutely not." Nash was emphatic.

"We could take you in for questioning you know."

Nash nodded. "Yes, you could."

"We could have your license."

"Yes, you could do that too."

The two policemen were studying him now. "It doesn't seem to worry you none."

"Friend, it doesn't bother me at all. I have a clean record, and nothing has passed between Hodgkins and myself that you could hang a complaint on. Still—I know that you could revoke the license on some excuse or other, if you decided to. But it's not very important."

"Whaddya mean by that crack? Without a license you can't do business."

"I haven't had enough business in the last year to fill a thimble; do with your license as you please. I don't have much use for it any more."

The second man spoke up with a new suspicion. "Are you thinking of moving?"

"I had considered it—yes."

"Where to?"

"I don't know. North, south, east, west—I don't know." He smiled blandly at the pair. "There isn't much for me to do in Knoxville any more."

The pair of officers lapsed into impatient silence, waiting for further questions to suggest themselves. Nash looked over their shoulders as the mortuary door opened again and the girl stepped out into the warm sunlight. She stopped just past the door to glance at Dikty, and then down the walk to where he waited with the police. Her eyes widened.

They were soft, dark brown eyes he noticed, almost the color of her smoothly brushed hair. Beside her, Dikty had turned his head to sniff curiously. The girl hesitated there but a second longer and then advanced along the walk, alone. Nash was sure that Dikty had whispered to her, had sent her away from him. She passed by the silent trio and continued up the street.

Nash smiled after her.

That would be Dikty's new secretary, Shirley Hoffman.

Shirley Hoffman was wearing a new perfume; Dikty had noted it and absently turned to sample the scent. Shirley Hoffman had recognized him standing there with the plain-clothes men and he had recognized her. She had changed perfumes but she wouldn't be able to change her voice.

Shirley Hoffman had been easy to find again.

Chapter 6

THE HOTELS were blanks.

The police had long since covered them all searching for Carolyn Hodgkins, and perhaps Dikty had visited them as well. Even a drastic change in the coloring of her hair as well as a change in name would not have concealed her, for the police would have examined the registers for those days immediately following her disappearance, would have carefully scrutinized each newcomer. And she could not alter the color of her eyes. The police would have likewise visited the bus and railway stations with her description, with the picture taken from the dresser top. Despite that, there remained the definite possibility she had slipped out of town without being seen. Carolyn Hodgkins was no bungling amateur.

Nash clasped his fingers beneath his chin, propped his elbows on the desk and considered her problem.

There were not too many places she *could* go that would be profitable for her; only Oak Ridge, Hanford, perhaps Brookhaven, and the Savannah River. That last brought a frown of speculation, Savannah River was processing heavy water. Carolyn Hodgkins might well go there. Or consider Los Alamos; Los Alamos might serve if she could sufficiently camouflage her real intentions, could present an acceptable reason for moving there. She just might meet another technician there who would serve her purpose, but her chances of marrying him were practically nil. Hodgkins's widow was a marked woman now, marked because she was a widow. Let even the suggestion of a marriage be broached in the proper circles and Los Alamos would trace the wife-to-be back through Oak Ridge and Knoxville all the way to that other marriage—that romantic meeting in the public library. She wouldn't want that, couldn't afford that. So Carolyn would not suggest marriage. The technician would be entertained without it.

Lucky fellow, he would think. Nash smiled to himself. Carolyn *did* have her points.

Now, she would pursue one of two goals, depending upon the mental schedule she had drawn up for herself. The star-ship would be launched from the Cape, or from Vandenberg in California, and so she would watch those pads for signs of increased activity. Or she had learned from her husband that the ship wasn't going up this year, and so would concentrate attention on one of the plants producing large quantities of heavy water. Nash wondered briefly if she had attempted to steal water—or was planning to steal some. She was desperate to the point where she would be willing to run any risk: she didn't want to die, she was afraid of dying.

And *that* was the fine point of distinction between the woman and himself. She was determined to live, to go back to the world of her birth, to take any risk to reach that world —but he had long ago decided to accept death on earth as it would come to him. He felt certain there was no returning.

Suddenly, Nash wondered just how many different projects Carolyn had had a finger in, during her life in *this* country?

Had she helped build the bomb? Going all the way back to the beginning, had she played a role in fashioning the atomic bomb? She knew only too well that no decent, durable ship could break out of the solar system without nuclear energy behind it—the various liquid fuels simply weren't enough, they did well to push men to the nearest planets and then bring them back. But to obtain that kind of energy for that kind of ship, the military had to come first. She was wise enough to know the military had to be made happy with a plaything of their own before other, peaceful applications would be permitted. *First* had to come the atomic reaction in an explosive, warlike form—any primitive government ruled by its military machine would insist on that. Next would come the commercial byproducts of manufacturing and huckstering, to placate the second ruling class from the top. After all that there would be exploration simply for the sake of knowledge. Science ran a poor last; it lacked the clout. All that was the pattern of human thinking, and Carolyn was aware of it.

Powder rockets were confined to the toys, to early warfare, and to amateur experimentation; the best of the powders couldn't propel a ship beyond ten thousand feet per second and the fuel was burned in a breath.

The various liquid combinations were only a little better, a bolsterer of hopes: kerosene and oxygen, gasoline, acetylene, even hydrogen and oxygen modified by borax distillate were but toddling steps, each one succeeding the other and each one pushing the next ship a few steps beyond the one just before it, but they weren't good enough for the stars. Nuclear energy was the only answer—short of a startling breakthrough in some unimaginable byway of physics—and Carolyn knew it. It was likely that she *had* poked and pried and rammed a finger in here and there, prodding Washington toward its first atomic bomb. Perhaps Gregg Hodgkins had delighted in erotic ways while she read his knowledge.

Perhaps she deftly inserted key ideas into his mind. She had been skilled in that art.

Given a worthy ship, and a reactor, the next step was a trustworthy line of communications to guide read, respond to, and oversee the vessel. Carolyn had moved to Knoxville and married a telemetry expert working on the Ridgerunner Project. Her personal project was very near completion, for that telemetric system built into the starship would be *more* than what Gregg Hodgkins had thought it would be.

Nash thought the woman's line of reasoning would be simple and direct. She was stubbornly determined to reach her goal—her own world.

Without her husband's knowledge or understanding she would cause him to build into the system some few provisions for her use alone. There would be a manual override, to permit her to break contact with earth base and guide the ship as she chose; there would be a circuit which would permit her to tap one of the message-repeater stations in deep space; and there would be a distress signal built into the vessel—a signal which would be heard by other ships, *her* kind of ships, traveling the starlanes.

Nash thought the circuit to tap the message-repeater stations was the most clever idea. And he wondered, too, what astronomers would think when they abandoned their present notions about quasars and build a suitable device for listening to them. *That* ought to shake up several scientific communities and a few of the more provincial governments.

He decided to stay in Knoxville only a little longer, searching for the widow. If he failed to find her in a week or two, Carolyn was on her way home.

If she remained here she would need housing; the hotels would be closed to her for purposes of secrecy after her husband's death—she would realize that. Likewise she would know—or guess—that someone would eventually get around to checking the real estate offices, searching for an apartment or house she may have rented after leaving that one hotel. And in Knoxville, apartments or houses weren't picked up in a day. What was it her husband had said? She began mentally packing and preparing to leave him several weeks prior to the date she actually walked out. Not only mentally packing, Nash decided. She had started moving, not a difficult thing to do when all she wanted or took were some of the contents of her bedroom.

Her closet space was empty, the vanity drawers empty. All the possessions she took with her could be packed into a trunk, and perhaps a suitcase on the side. And she had thoughtfully secured a place to move *to* long before the day she deserted her husband, so many months before that a routine check today would reveal nothing suspicious. *Sudden thought:* to the home of that hypothetical third party?

To move that trunk she would have hired a taxi or a small delivery truck. She would avoid the risk of having a third party call for her, having him seen by neighbors. If that third party existed, both he and Carolyn could go to the extreme to conceal his existence.

Nash unlocked his fingers, stood up, stretched.

The afternoon hours were growing late and dusk would not be long in coming. A few short hours ago Hodgkins had made his last public appearance; since the services Nash had done nothing but lounge in his office, brooding. Now he put on his coat, closed the window, tested the door latch with his thumb and stepped out into the corridor.

Knoxville's streets were full of homebound crowds.

Gilbert Nash selected a nearby restaurant, preferring to eat downtown because he thought it too early to go home, too early to separate himself from the noisy company of people. After a short wait in the closely packed place, he was given a small booth in the back, and ordered an ale to pass the time until the meal would be ready. Idly, he scanned the people surging about the room.

Shirley Hoffman entered the door, made a small face when she discovered the waiting line and hopelessly searched for a vacant table. She saw Nash a moment later and her eyes widened involuntarily, as they had done earlier that afternoon. She made a tentative move as if to leave.

Nash was on his feet in an instant, inviting her to join him with a gesture and a welcoming smile. She stepped out of the line, paused to express doubt with a frown, and then slowly threaded her way among the tables to where he waited. Her face still wore a hint of indecision.

His smile dissolved into a wide grin. "If it's that bad, go away. I'll withdraw the invitation."

"No, please." She apologized and slid into the seat opposite his. "Really, it isn't what you must be thinking at all. But—"

"But what? Out with it."

"You *must* think I followed you here. I did catch a glimpse of you on the street a moment ago, but I didn't follow you. I often eat here."

"Glad to know it," Nash reassured her, "and I'll come back again." He continued to grin across the table at her, to put her at ease.

"But tell me just one thing and I'll answer your doubts. You recognized me this afternoon?"

"Yes."

"I thought so. I'm pleased to meet you. My name is Gilbert Nash and yours is Shirley Hoffman."

"How did you . . . ?" She stopped and fought away a blush of confusion, her eyes avoiding his. "I suppose it *is* rather silly to pretend we don't know each other."

"It is, yes. And I like the sound of your voice."

Her glance flew back to his, startled and wondering.

Nash was still grinning, almost laughing at her. "Dikty betrayed you, there in the doorway. He didn't recognize the new perfume you're wearing. I like it though." He waited a moment to reassure her. "I told you I'd find you again."

Her answering words rushed out hotly. "And now I suppose you're going to ask me what I was doing there!"

"No—I'm not. I know we were both there for the same reason: information. And I know that we both gained the same amount: nothing. You came away with just one thing I did not, and vice versa."

She waited for him to continue, not speaking.

He flicked a casual finger at her purse on the table. "You have a key, I have a hairpin." And then suddenly he grinned again. "But I knew you didn't have a gun last night. I only pretended you had one."

Hoffman bit her lip, cautiously watching him, and then quickly laughed. "So did I."

The waitress stopped at their table.

"I'm having steak. Want an ale while you're waiting?"

"Yes, to both," she answered. "Gilbert Nash, you're a most curious man. I've never met anyone quite like you."

"That," he replied dryly, "is the opening gambit to a thousand flatteries, coming from anyone else I'd call it a thousand and one. But you, you can't help yourself. Dikty's job rubs off on you."

"Oh, now, I didn't intend . . ."

"I know you didn't, so don't apologize. And I don't mind in the least. Dikty and I have been keeping our weather eyes on each other for a long time. Amusing, eh?"

"I'm sorry," she said sincerely, "but we may as well be frank about this, don't you think?"

"Do, yes. There's no point at all in going along and pretending that he isn't watching me, every move I make. He'll have a report on this meal before morning." Nash chuckled.

"But I don't believe *he* could sit down with me like this and enjoy dinner; he's too much the formal, hidebound Sherlock." He glanced across the table at her, amusement in tone and gesture. "I think you can."

"I think so too. And how are you, Mr. Nash?"

"Splendid, Miss Hoffman."

"You sent me to the library this morning."

"I did? That's curious—it must have been something I said. Probably last night."

She nodded. "It was. You were speaking of hairpins. You said 'you may fashion it into the horns of a bull and hold it over a flame.' I wondered what you meant by that."

"Yes. I remember it now. That was in the nature of a spark. If you had been who I first thought you were, last night, that would have started a fire."

"Really?" She stared at him with round curious eyes. "You must have been expecting Mrs. Hodgkins?"

He nodded and sipped the ale.

"How would *that* have started a fire? I mean—what does it mean? I couldn't find a thing at the library to offer a hint; I must have driven the poor librarian crazy. We searched the black magic and voodoo shelves from one end to the other. You see, I thought you might be a male witch. But there was nothing concerning the horns of a bull."

Nash laughed gaily, causing some of the nearer diners to turn and look. "Wrong department of research. Next time try archeology—and in particular the Middle East and the Mediterranean. Bulls were employed as sacrifices, as ornaments, and as strange partners in erotic dances in ancient Crete; the customs and habits occasionally spilled over into the surrounding states." He whooped again. "Male witch!"

"And you were there!" she retorted flippantly.

"I've been there," Nash answered.

"Oh? Teacher, archeologist?"

"Let's say, as a student, an ambulant armchair archeologist, but I did go over the ground. Never had the opportunity to actually participate in the digging, but I would have liked to. One of my many hobbies—I enjoy studying anything having to do with people. I have a fair-sized collection of books on the subject and some few artifacts; I enjoy comparing the volumes against each other, pairing off the learned scholars in opinionated battle. Consider those Cretan bulls for example. One authority would have us believe they were sacrifices to a god and that youths would perform ritual dances around them as they were led away —a sort of farewell party. But another scholar will stoutly maintain that the youths were sacrifices to the bulls—they were dancing and cavorting about before meeting their deaths. Can you imagine cavorting with joy at your own funeral? But still another will say it was nothing more than an acrobatic act, a skilled performance for an audience, similar to modern bullfighting.

"One can't blame these writers too much—they have so little to go on. *This* particular incident is based on a few paintings and carved rings uncovered at the sites. And Victorian man, if you need reminding, is apt to interpret things and events according to his reasoning and logic, still believing he is following the logic of antiquity."

"But, which is right?" Hoffman asked curiously.

"None, really. At least in ancient Crete. Our scholars readily realized that the dancers were of both sexes, and always fair and young. But our scholars are cursed with modern minds. They weren't quick to realize—or at least admit—that the affairs were purely erotic in nature. Performed for an audience. That's rather foreign to present-day thinking. So the archeologists lean to the sacrificial explanation, although I'll admit their thinking is colored by other finds. In later times the dances spilled over into the other Aegean islands and degenerated into brawl and senseless murder." He caught her sudden expression. "You think my choice of words poor, or is it my sense of values? You could be right, whichever; but I don't always manage to keep pace with changing values. I do think the original purposes of the rites were lofty, compared to the blood lusts that followed. The morals of one age are not those of the next."

She was silent, considering all that he had said while the waitress prepared the table. She hoped her thoughts weren't too apparent on her face. When they were alone again she closed one eye and fixed him with a semiserious glance. "You sound as though you *were* there."

"A healthy imagination," he answered dryly, "plus an undying curiosity about all things human from the time your Paleolithic ancestors first began piling one stone atop another to build a wall, up to and including the ships that leap into the sky—yesterday, today and tomorrow. I want to know where man came from, what he has been doing all these years, and where he is going. Especially where he is going."

"My favorite grandmother," she interposed, "used to say we were going to hell in a bucket."

"In one language or another, they've said that for five thousand years. Don't believe it."

"I know a man," she copied his dry tone, "who is interested in your interest."

"Good! Send him around someday and we'll have a first-rate bull session—no pun intended. I'll do my best to amuse him. Does he have an interest in archeology? Is he a religious man? Maybe he'd like to hear about the religious uproar in England when an indiscreet Englishman found evidence of a tremendous deluge."

"I rather doubt it," Hoffman shook her head, the brown hair swirling. "His interests run along other lines. But I'll listen."

"You can't very well help yourself!" Nash plunked down the ale bottle on the tabletop. "The steaks aren't ready and

you're trapped. More ale? You don't mind if I do? Thanks.
Well . . . our Englishman was excavating in Mesopotamia,
delving into Assyrian and Babylonian history for traces
of a still earlier people who had handed down to them a
form of writing. Did you know that the source of the
world's first form of writing is still unknown?"

"I'm not very bright. What about the Englishman?"

"Still digging—he made several finds on the site, finds of
immense scientific value and of course much gold. It's a
curious thing, but do you know, you humans worship gold
above knowledge? Without exception, every archeologist
I've heard or read of has discovered gold in his graves and
excavations, and has attached as much or more importance
to that than the artifacts he found there. Let one of them
make a report of a new find, and at the early beginning of
that report he will give a description of the gold leaves,
gold headdresses, gold this or gold that that he uncovered.
I think that curious."

He paused to see if she even remotely agreed with him.

"The deluge," Hoffman reminded him.

"To be sure—the deluge. Well there he was, this Englishman, spading around and turning up first one thing and
another, until finally he chanced upon a mass grave of roy-
alty and servants. The ladies in waiting, the soldiers, the
slaves, all murdered at the graveside and unceremoniously
dumped in with their masters. That was highly unusual at
that particular place and time, so the Englishman dug
deeper. Beneath the mass grave he discovered a layer of
thick yellow clay eight feet through, and below *that*, there
were still other remains of humans and building. So there
you are."

"So there I am not!" she contradicted him. "What is it
all about?"

Nash seemed mildly surprised. "The eight-foot layer of
clay," he said matter-of-factly, "deposited by an immense

flood, accompanied by high winds and rivers running out of their banks. Forty days and forty nights of rain, one hundred and fifty days before the waters receded—all that left an eight-foot deposit in the valley between the Tigris and the Euphrates. The Biblical flood, pretty well pinned down. Human remains above the clay as well as below it. Our Englishman left the religious world in something of a turmoil. They didn't quite appreciate the show."

"Now you're running in more Englishmen on me," she complained. "You aren't fair!"

"But haven't you heard of the Gilgamesh Epic?"

"Gilgamesh?" she repeated. "No."

Nash shook his head, sadly reproving her. "Modern woman, tch, tch."

"Oh tch, tch, my eye! All right, I'm thoroughly trapped now. Tell me about the other two Englishmen and the Gilgamesh Epic. Will this be a short story?"

"Sort of. I'll condense it. These other two Englishmen came before the one we just finished off. The *first* one found and shipped home to England several tablets dug out of a buried palace. The *second* Englishman then spent several years and all but wrecked his health in translating those tablets, seeking to confirm certain theories proposed by the man before. His translation rocked the staid Victorians and created the hubbub. The poor fellow was not fully vindicated until our *third* Englishman happened along some years later and discovered that bed of clay beneath the mass grave and the palaces."

Hoffman nodded brightly. "The point is slowly becoming clear. The translator found a Biblical story on the clay tablets."

Nash regarded her with speculation. "No. He found what was supposed to be a work of pure fiction."

"Supposed to be?"

He nodded, smiling faintly. "A poem of epic proportions. The tablets had been taken from an ancient king's library, you must understand, along with many others of a more common nature. Those others contained the usual factual data and were more or less expected: histories, genealogical studies, accounts of wards, of great personages, of prisoners and booty taken, some crude geographical surveys—everything a king might desire to make his library a storehouse of knowledge and of course a testimony to his own greatness. Now comes the square peg for the round hole. That library also contained this panoramic poem, in an age where fiction (if you'll pardon the modern term) was almost unknown. This was a poem of a heroic, marvelous character—a godlike man called Gilgamesh."

"Oh . . ." Hoffman broke in, parted her lips to speak and then changed her mind. She watched him closely.

"He was a man whose beginnings, whose origin were either unknown or unrecorded, and who stalked through the land accomplishing mighty deeds. Gilgamesh was something of a born adventurer who roamed the entire known world at that time, seeking knowledge, seeking immortality. He appeared here, visited there, upsetting tyrants and unsettling kingdoms. He finally met up with a prehistoric man with an unpronounceable name and . . ."

"*How* unpronounceable?" she interrupted.

"Ut-napishtim."

Hoffman nodded her agreement. "Unpronounceable."

". . . And that fellow told Gilgamesh the story of *his* life," Nash continued. He looked over at the girl musingly. "Come to think of it, that was probably the first use of the flashback technique in history. Imagine that—a fictioneer of forty centuries ago invented the flashback."

Hoffman cupped her chin in her hand. "Gilgamesh . . ."

"I'm getting there! So the prehistoric man told Gilgamesh an incredible tale that dwarfed any of his own adventures. He told of a terrible flood that descended upon the world, told of his building a boat and loading it with supplies, loading it with all the animals he could gather, and the calling aboard of his kinfolk from far and near. He told how his little ship had courageously ridden through the storm and rising waters for many days and nights, and finally, how he sent out first a dove and then a raven to seek land. And that was how Ut-napishtim and his clan lived through the deluge while all around them perished." Nash studied the girl over the rim of his glass. "Sound familiar?"

"*That* was on the clay tablets?" she demanded.

"It was. Hammered out as pure fiction."

"And the tablets were supposed to be how old?"

"Three to four thousand years. Do you see now why the Victorians suddenly suffered rising blood pressure?"

"Indeed I do! I should be inclined to doubt the evidence myself. But I suppose this is where our third Englishman comes in?"

"Does, yes. He showed that the tablets were indeed fiction. They were the Assyrian version of hand-me-down Babylonian tales, which in turn were presumably based on fact. Simply a case of one kingdom borrowing a neighbor's folk history and concocting a story. The Englishman made several discoveries indicating the authenticity of the tablets, including that layer of clay deposited by the flood. So you see—even historical novels, superman novels, were written four thousand years ago. Knocked out in clay. The skeptic may regard this one as merely a tale told by some nameless poet who sought to please a king, the believer, as the bold and earliest chronicler of Noah." His fingers drummed on the tabletop. "If you put any faith in archeology at all, you will find that excavators have not only discovered and dated the deluge, but have gone on to discover traces of a still earlier people who must have lived in the times of Genesis. They are slowly catching up with anthropology and geology."

"I'm curious about the dates," Hoffman said, just as curiously watching him.

"The deluge? Well, our Englishman's mass burial of king and slave happened about six thousand years ago. The layer of clay was before that, beneath it. Eight, ten thousand years ago? That remains to be seen. What you call modern man has been on earth now some million years and your primitive ancestor existed for perhaps another million before that. That's a rather broad span in which to attempt to pin down a definite place and time, but men are still digging. One group in particular is now searching for old Ut-napishtim's boat. If and when they find it, they can pretty well date it. Or rather, they can date the trees which furnished timber for the boat."

"I've heard of that," the girl put in. "Tree rings."

"No—not in a case like this. Someone has come up with a new process of measurement called the C-14 method, a process which measures the passage of time by the amount of radioactive residue in an organic substance. Your tree rings would be useless here because the tree died when it was cut down. It might measure life before it was felled, but not after." He paused a moment in thought. "If the archeologists are lucky enough to find a chunk of wood from Ut-napishtim's boat—well, they will tell you the approximate year that tree stood. The approximate year of Noah and his flood." He grinned mischievously. "I wonder if that information will upset anyone?"

They lapsed into silence as the waitress brought the meal and served it. Shirley Hoffman absently watched the woman lay out the dishes, fiddle with the silver, watched Nash spread a napkin in his lap. The room continued to be filled with noisy humanity. She looked up from the napkin to his face, to his eyes which startled her each time she saw them.

"I want to ask one more question," she ventured after a

moment. "You very briefly mentioned the subject but you neglected to follow it through."

He stopped a bite of steak on its way to his mouth. "What was that?"

"Did this adventurer, this Gilgamesh fellow, find his immortality?"

Nash held the fork poised in mid-air for a moment and then slowly slipped the meat into his mouth. After a second's hesitation he glanced at the girl's intent face.

"He found what he was searching for. But it was much too late to save his life."

Chapter 7

CUMMINGS WANDERED in aimless circles about the inner office, looking for pictures on the wall that had never been there, absently seeking a splotch of sunlight on the floor that had not yet arrived with the early morning sun. He hesitated at the window, gloomily streaked his finger through the dust on the sill and then put his head out into the warm air to search the sky. The sun was still hidden behind the building. An interested pigeon perched on a nearby ledge, returning his curious stare. He blinked at the pigeon and pulled his head in, conscious that there might be others above him.

"He talks to horses," Cummings said dourly to the man seated at the desk behind him.

Dikty nodded in assent. "Apparently."

"He *must* talk to the horses; they're his friends. They tell him when and where to place his money—as if *they* knew which one was going to win! He scares me. The people over at Treasury tell me he's something unique; he carefully notes down all his winnings but never his losses. Uusally, it's the other way around. If they remember to include this gambling at all. But Treasury claims his tax returns are models of something or other; fifty dollars for this case, seventy-five for that one, total earnings as an investigator something less than a thousand per year. You'd think he would starve."

"But he doesn't apparently," Dikty murmured.

"He doesn't!" Cummings kicked at a chair in disgust. "Thanks to his friends, the horses. His tax returns are the damn'dest things I've ever seen in my life. His habit is to attach a typed letter to each one, naming the tracks, the horses, the dates, the odds, and the amounts of his winnings. Twenty-odd thousand dollars last year if you believe it! Treasury does; they don't even bother to check up on him any more—they know he's right. When the returns first started coming in some field office got curious and checked a few dates; they followed his luck pretty closely for two or three years. Now, they're happy that he doesn't deduct his losses, if any. If any, Dikty! The horses *must* talk to him."

"A shrewd cover," Dikty commented. "A very shrewd cover for an income of less than a thousand per year. That house out in the country is costing him something. Say— when was the first year he filed?"

"March of 1941, for the previous year. In Georgia." Cummings continued his distracted pacing of the room. "I've put a bug in their ear; they've started some discreet snooping, checking his bank account, checking the pay-off windows at those tracks he mentioned. With his fantastic luck, *some* of those parimutuel clerks must remember him. Well, we'll see." He glanced impatiently at his watch. "Want to catch the plane for Louisville at noon; it's the usual rough going up at that new plant on the river." The pacing had brought him to the doorway between the inner and outer offices. He stared around the vacant outer room and then back to Dikty. "The girl's not in yet."

"Something holding her up I suspect."

"Sick?"

"Landlady said no." Dikty retrieved his pipe from an inner

pocket. "Landlady said she left an hour or more ago, in a devil of a hurry. She'll be along."

Cummings turned back to the window. "She had dinner with him last night, eh? Maybe he gave her a tip on a horse."

"I'm the fool who did the tipping," Dikty retorted sourly, staring into the black bowl of the pipe. "Subject connected the two of us at the funeral when he saw me sniffing her perfume. I thought it was something new and stopped to sniff—it was. But she stumbled onto him in a restuarant last night and he promptly invited her to his table. She jumped at the opportunity. Reports that he made no attempt at all to pump her—it was the other way around."

"She'll do," Cummings nodded, searching the sky. He put his head out once more to find his feathered friend still there, still watching him. Contemplating the pigeon, Cummings asked, "Pick up anything on the microphones?"

Dikty said no. "Not a blessed thing. He returned to his office after the Hodgkins funeral and spent the entire afternoon reading—apparently. No sounds but chair, desk, shoes, paper, the usual thing. He doesn't even talk to himself out loud." Dikty reached into a vest pocket and extracted a slip of paper. "He stopped by a bookstore this morning to order a book. *The Thermodynamics of the Steady State*. That's not politics—I asked. Something to do with chemical engineering."

"Subject's healthy interest in science continues."

Dikty packed his pipe in silence and then poised an unlit match in the air. "I've been wondering if it could have anything to do with Code four-four-seven? Chemical engineering now. But then, I'm suspicious of everything and everybody."

"I don't know; I sort of doubt it, but I'll look into it." Cummings shook his head. "You can never be sure until you've checked. We had to stop the presses on an encyclopedia last week—the fools were going to publish the figures on the critical mass of U-235."

"A man worked it out! The consulting physicist who was writing the article for them figured it out in his fool head, and wanted to include it. We also made him eliminate some references to the refining properties of U-238; he wanted to tell the world how to make a more potent explosion. We seized the plates and several thousand copies already run off. How long can this go on?"

Dikty didn't answer because the outer door opened then and Shirley Hoffman staggered in, her arms laden with dusty volumes. Her eager young face seemed excited.

"Good morning," she said brightly, looking from one to the other. "I've been to the library. Treasure trove." She pushed the corridor door shut with her heel and dropped the burden on her desk. "Heavy work."

Cummings gravely examined the stack of books and then glanced at Dikty. "Frittering away her time with reading. Don't you keep her busy?"

"Bosh," Hoffman cut in before Dikty could think of an answer. "I'm hot on the trail."

"Of what?"

"Of mummies, buried kings, the deluge, and Gilgamesh." She paused a moment in frowning thought. "Gilgamesh can't be found. Not in our library."

"I'll get it for you in Washington," Cummings said, and in the next breath added, "Why?"

"Told you I was hot on the trail! Our subject knows all about Gilgamesh, so I want to know all about Gilgamesh." She thought to correct the supervisor. "Gilgamesh is a him, not an it. A prehistoric man who wandered around the ancient Mediterranean; he's in archeology. Can you really get it for me?"

"I don't believe there are more than nine million books

in the Library of Congress." He snapped his fingers. "You
name it and you can have it. Just like that."

"Now you're making fun of me."

Cummings turned again to examine the stack of volumes.
"And now it's archeology?"

"Yes, very much so. It was all he talked about last night
and he wasn't merely trying to impress me. He knew. I
shouldn't be surprised to find he knows things that aren't in
these books."

Dikty grunted. "He knows which horse is the winner."

A door slammed with a distant, muffled sound and the
three of them ceased talking. Dikty twisted around in his
chair to reach out and touch the volume control on a tiny
speaker mounted on his desk. The speaker hummed with
increased life, but nothing more. The trio waited long minutes in continued silence.

"Subject has reported for work," Dikty muttered after a
while. "Busy making his thousand or less for this year." He
listened as the microphone picked up new sounds, the
muffled footsteps crossing a distant floor, a window being
raised, a chair being pulled away from a desk. A heavy
squeaking as the chair was occupied. And then nothing.

"Serious thinker," Cummings suggested dryly.

"He is, really," Hoffman agreed. "He has the detached
viewpoint of the scholar, the witness who is sitting out of the
mainstream of history, merely appraising it as it marches by.
He continually referred to *my* ancestors, *my* humans, as if
they were mine but not his."

"He had to be born somewhere," Dikty repeated his old
declaration. "And I don't mean in Miami, Florida on
March 8th, 1940. After all—he's sixty years old now."

"Apparently," Cummings murmured. He was at the window again, watching the pigeon.

Dikty threw him a suspicious glance.

"I rather like him," Hoffman quickly interposed. "He is a funny man. By that I mean strange. Strange eyes, strange skin, strange manner of thinking. Sometimes I could glimpse the thought behind his speech—very strange thoughts. I found myself wondering if he thought in words, in pictures, in symbols or abstractions; perhaps he doesn't think the way we do at all. But I rather like him."

"Don't," Cummings warned suddenly, whirling from the window. "And be careful! Have you read the reports—oh, yes, you typed them. Well, study them carefully, and be careful of him. Until we or the police turn up a proven murderer, he's our suspect—a double suspect for loitering about the Ridge." He turned to Dikty. "What was it he said to the police yesterday? After the funeral?"

"That he was thinking of moving, that there isn't much left for him in Knoxville any more."

"If I thought for a moment he was referring to Hodgkins, I'd nab him now! But he seems to have another purpose now—he's hunting the Hodgkins widow."

"Who isn't?"

Cummings again caught sight of the books stacked atop the girl's desk. "Why these," he asked curiously, "why this—this what's-his-name man?"

"Gilgamesh. Partly to satisfy my curiosity," she hastened to explain, "and partly to catch him in an error. If *that's* possible. He told me things last night about history (or prehistory rather) that I never dreamed existed, and I'm very eager to learn more. He also told me things that may not be in these books and if that be the case . . ." She let the suggestion hang there.

"If that be the case, we know more than we know less about him." He flipped open a cover to read the flyleaf.

"Do you know about something or other called the C-14 method?" Shirley asked.

Cummings shut the book to study her. "Yes. An atomic

measurement of time, a by-product of the Ridge you might say. Why?"

"He said, if they find the remains of old Noah's Ark, they can measure the passage of time since it was built."

"That's right."

Dikty laughed aloud, a short, chopped, nasty laugh. "Now I've got an idea! Let's cut off one of his fingers and measure *his* age."

"That's revolting," Hoffman declared.

Cummings turned completely around and then stopped. "Dikty . . ." he said, thumping the topmost book, "Dikty . . ."

"Oh now really," the girl protested. "That's going too far!"

Cummings silenced her with one swift glare. "Dikty," he repeated, "if our subject *should* turn up dead, if something unfortunate *should* happen to him, well, you grab that corpse, quick!"

Dikty nodded, slightly astonished that his bad joke had contained a grim morsel of merit. Shirley Hoffman held her shocked silence, sensing the rebuke the supervisor had thrown at her. His callous suggestion had unnerved her.

"I don't believe in passing up anything," Cummings continued, "no matter how insignificant or ridiculous it may seem on the surface. That is why our outfit is in the high and tight position we occupy today. And inasmuch as we can't locate his date and place of birth, we—oh, my God!"

"What's the matter?" Dikty was on his feet in alarm.

"Hodgkins's wife—I mean widow. We couldn't find her birth date or birthplace either. When she married Hodgkins she had no past!"

Dikty lost only a second in absorbing the statement and then sat down again, to scrabble frantically through the papers in a desk drawer. He finally found those he was searching for and ran his eyes rapidly down the typed lines, coming to rest on two long paragraphs. He read the paragraphs a second time and then looked up at his superior.

"According to the police and the neighbors, a part of the descriptions match: the unusual eyes, the posed swift lines, the long youthfulness . . ."

Cummings hesitated only a moment longer, his face now tightened into a harsh knot of speculative thought, and then he grabbed up his hat. "That plane—" He sped for the outer door.

"Don't forget Gilgamesh," Hoffman called after him.

"What?" Cummings jerked around.

"Gilgamesh—my prehistoric man."

He threw her a fleeting, curious stare and was gone. The corridor door slammed shut behind him.

"I think," Dikty said quietly, "that something is about to happen to our friend."

Chapter 8

NASH HAD SLOWLY become aware that someone was following him.

The disturbing shadow lurking somewhere behind was not the security agent, Dikty. Dikty's habitual spying on him the past few weeks had easily resolved into a predictable pattern, had become a familiar and routine thing, a known presence he could almost sense whenever the man took up the trail behind him. Dikty would occasionally slip and allow himself to be glimpsed in a mirror, a store window, allow himself to be seen on an abrupt about-face. Dikty knew that Nash was aware of his presence and accepted it; the motions of secrecy were maintained because that was part of the game, but the actual secrecy had been abandoned when each realized the other was aware of the situation.

And now—this new shadow.

It was not Dikty behind him; Dikty was ahead of him. This day, Gilbert Nash had quietly and with some amusement turned the tables and begun following Dikty, for he saw that the security agent was intent upon Hodgkins's widow. Nash plodded along behind Dikty, following him on the rounds of several banks, the various utility offices, numberless real estate brokers and some of the automobile agencies. Doubtless the police had already gone over a part or all of the ground during their routine search of the hotels and transportation depots, but still Dikty must go over it again, and Nash curiously followed to see what he might turn up. Hour after hour of the hot afternoon went by and still Dikty searched fruitlessly, still Nash tagged along after him, and still the strange new shadow hung behind them both.

It was not the girl on his trail—Nash realized that. Shirley Hoffman played a different game, had played it well since the day of the funeral. She was not expert enough to keep completely hidden as the stranger was doing, not well enough versed in the art of stalking a man to avoid reflections in store windows, to avoid being caught flat-footed by a quick stop or a turnaround. Too, she would never excel at tailing and roping because there was about her person an aura which gave her away. Her perfume may have been a part of it, or her personality, or the mental activity she exuded; but she could not hide herself. Nash would suddenly realize she was somewhere near, would walk around a corner or pass through a doorway and she would be there. It was a compelling, magnetic quality that advertised her presence in advance.

But that was the way she played the game. Instead of attempting to hide from him she placed herself where she might be seen, where he might chance upon her as by accident, stop to talk, and end by inviting her to spend an evening. They had dined together several times and twice had gone to a concert; once she offered to take him to a movie but he declined, disliking the idea of wasting several hours in a theater watching a picture he didn't care for.

Nash stopped in a drugstore, ordered ice cream, and sat down on a stool where he could watch the doorway of the real estate office across the street. Dikty in his fashion and Hoffman in hers—they had certainly taken an intent interest

in him. He grinned briefly. They were unmistakably preparing to close in. And now the new tail.

Idly, he watched the people going by outside the window, wondering if one of them might be his new shadow.
A young man sauntering along with a briefcase, two women
with packages in their hands and inspecting each window as
they passed it, a gangling youth reading a science fiction
magazine, a man, another man, a young woman, another
man, two boys carrying empty newspaper bags, an old fellow wearing a battered straw hat, a man with a briefcase—
Nash jerked his eyes around to follow the repeater. Briefcase entered the drugstore and bought a package of pipe
tobacco. He did not reappear. The parade continued past
the window. Dikty emerged from the doorway across the
street. Nash finished his ice cream and strolled outside, letting Dikty have the lead of a full block. As soon as he left
the drugstore he again felt the presence of eyes behind
him, on him.

The invisible eyes were disconcerting, malignant. They
imparted a sense of unease and irritation because they could
not be located and identified, because they constantly bored
into the back of his head like a telescopic sight on a rifle.
Again and again he attempted to locate them without visibly advertising his intention, but without success. The man
was damned slick—whoever he was. He briefly considered
Dikty's superior officer, Cummings; it could be Cummings.
Or it could be a new man Cummings had assigned to the
city.

Dikty continued his hopeless search for some hint or
trace of the widow, possibly aware of Nash behind him or
possibly not, but Nash was certain he did not feel the new
shadow there or he would certainly have done something
about it. *Sudden thought:* Dikty might know very well a
new man was behind the two of them, and so ignored the
matter. In any event, Dikty went on looking for some scrap

of information that might point out the hiding place of Hodgkins's widow, but looked for nothing behind him.

Nash grinned to himself once more as a wry thought struck him. Suppose, just suppose, that every detective or spy or secret agent or whatever authority or source wore some sort of identifying badge or clothing—a long red cloak perhaps, wouldn't it be a ridiculous sight for the townspeople to see Dikty slipping along the street in his flapping red cloak, to see Nash tripping along behind him in his, and then by merely turning their heads, to see a third party sneaking along in the rear! A regular parade of spies, each following the other. With now and then perhaps a local plain-clothes man standing idly on some street corner, watching the crowds and watching the first three pussyfooting along.

Nash laughed aloud.

Late in the afternoon, Dikty's trail led past the public library and Nash felt the sudden intuition that Shirley Hoffman was nearby. He abandoned Dikty and turned in the double doors. She was checking out some books at the desk. Nash walked up beside her, watched the librarian punch Hoffman's card and number through the dating machine, and reached over to pick them up.

"*The Oldest Civilization of Greece,*" he read after flipping the uppermost column spine-up. "Badly out-dated; fifty years old if it's a day."

The librarian looked at him with disapproval.

"Hello," Hoffman smiled. "You have newer, I suppose?"

"Have yes. Want to go out and look at them?"

"I'm willing—although I suppose I should have hesitated modestly."

Nash laughed. "A book has never raped anyone yet."

The librarian glared.

Hoffman turned with flushed face and made for the door. Outside she paused. "Now, how can I go back in there and face that woman?"

"Oh, she didn't mind what I said. It was the noise I was making."

"I can just imagine!" Hoffman retorted, her voice reflecting the fast-fading indignation. "It will be days . . . Oh, I *do* have something here." She fingered the books he was carrying and removed one from the stack. "The librarian recommended it after I outlined my wants: Huxley's *After Many a Summer Dies the Swan.*"

He stared at it curiously. "Why that?"

"I asked for anything on longevity or immortality."

Nash stopped walking and turned to look at her. People darted impatiently around the small island-obstacle they created on the sidewalk. "Still riding Gilgamesh?"

Hoffman nodded determinedly. "Still Gilgamesh. Mr. Cummings is sending something from Washington."

"But this isn't the same," he protested, tapping the volume in her hands. "This is a dying old man who is determined not to die; he's willing to spend every million he has to stay alive forever."

"Does he?" she wanted to know, examining the worn cover of the book.

"That's the fine point of the story; read it and see. You'll have to wade through sermons knee-deep, but see for yourself." He began walking again.

"But he and Gilgamesh were after the same thing," she protested.

"Yes—in a sense. This old man was fifty or sixty years old and afraid to die because he was also afraid of meeting God face to face. But Gilgamesh was something else altogether. Gilgamesh was—well, *much* older, and sought only to prolong his life its natural span, to live out his appointed time. Much the way you would ward off a childhood disease, then you might live to be an adult. He was not afraid of dying, nor afraid to meet his God; when he realized his search for 'immortality' was a useless one he abandoned it, resigned himself to dying young." Nash gave her a sidelong glance. "That's a relative term; not young in the sense that you are young."

Hoffman moved her head to catch his eye. "And how young are you?" she asked bluntly.

"Over twenty-one," he answered promptly and laughed. "I learned that from women who vote."

"Cheat!" she declared.

"Nosey," he replied.

They walked slowly with the evening crowd, making no attempt to match its speed and bound nowhere in particular. People hurried past them intent upon their many individual destinations, upon their personal futures. After a silence the girl spoke again.

"How old was Gilgamesh?"

"When?"

"Oh—when he met Noah, for instance."

"I would say many hundreds of years."

"Really?" She thought about it for a moment. "Then he would be several thousand today."

Nash inclined his head. "Would, yes."

"But that's quite impossible!"

"Yes, isn't it."

She looked up at him with mild irritation. "You are saying that just to agree with me, not because you believe it. No one lives to be several thousand years old."

"Remind me to tell you about the May flies—later on this evening when I have you in my web."

"May flies? What in the world do they have to do with Gilgamesh?"

"They live a full lifetime in less than a day," he said.

"Oh? Your implication then, is that a year in the life of Gilgamesh is not the same as a year in my life."

"Yes and no; again, the terms are relative."

"But would Gilgamesh *still* say he was dying young?"

"If he were alive today, yes."

"Why?"

"Because he would be—far short of his old age."

"But why," she persisted. "Why would he be dying? What was it that he was seeking to prolong his life?"

Nash grinned down at her in high humor. "Those buried tablets didn't say. The old poet gave no hint."

Irritation welled up within her again, but she fought to conceal it. She changed the subject. "Where shall we eat? I'm hungry. We are going to eat, aren't we?"

"Spoken like a forward wench. Dine them and wine them well, then invite them in to see the etchings." He laughed aloud and a passing few turned to stare at him. Taking her arm, he guided her across the sidewalk. "Can you cook?"

"Certainly. I expect to be married someday."

"Let's practice this evening."

"Cooking, or being married?"

"Hoffman!" He removed his hand from her arm.

"I suppose," she said expectantly, "that you have the usual well-equipped kitchen?"

"Have, yes. My car's not far from here." He moved a single step and then stopped again, quite suddenly. His attitude was one of intent listening. The pedestrian current flowed around them.

Hoffman glanced up at him, turned to follow his blank gaze and instantly mistook his intentions. He was staring absently at a florist's display window, now lighted up for the coming darkness. She thought he was examining the window.

"Flowers?" she asked with surprise. "Are you becoming serious?"

"What?" he replied, inattentive. He was still listening to something unseen, unknown. In the previous instant he had realized that the eyes were gone, the telescopic sights removed from the back of his head. He knew it as surely as though he had seen the man stop, remove the flapping red cloak with a flourish, and walk off home. Thinking back quickly, he realized now that the boring eyes had left him when he entered the library, but had not been there again when he emerged with the girl.

And that implied—what?

That the eyes knew the girl was waiting in the library— waiting for him, and she would take up the surveillance for the remainder of the evening? Or had those eyes not been interested in him at all but were really following Dikty? Had they rested so long on the cut of his hair merely because he happened to be in direct line of sight between Dikty and the unknown shadow? But why would those eyes be interested in Dikty? Dikty was not a threat to their hallowed security. Or perhaps—when *he* ceased trailing Dikty, it was no longer necessary for the eyes to follow him. Was the girl expected to watch for the night, or would there be another when she left him? Had they begun a twenty-four-hour watch over him? If they had, it was past time to start moving; they were surely preparing to close in.

"Gilbert Nash!" the girl exclaimed.

He emerged from his inner shell. "What?"

"I said the florist is closed."

That escaped him for a second or so until his glance came to rest on the illuminated window, and he guessed her thoughts. "Oh, too bad," he answered. "And I wanted to buy you a cactus. Come on, let's find my car. I'm curious as to how well you can cook."

Nash moved his chair back from the table and patted his stomach, his lips making a contented sound. He winked across the table at the girl and closed his eyes.

"Behold," Shirley Hoffman declared, "the well-stuffed male! One would think you'd never eaten catfish and hush puppies before." She placed an elbow on the table and propped her chin in the palm of her hand. "And now, if you're running true to form, you want to take a nap."

"*Negra consentida;* you speak like experience."

"I've had experience with my boss and male relatives. And that means what?"

"My pet brunette. After tonight, you are. Any woman who can prepare a meal like that *is* my pet."

"Any woman," she repeated. "I'm only the latest."

"The latest *and* the first, in this house at least. It would surprise you to know how long it has been since I've enjoyed a woman's company." He chuckled. "My good neighbors will have a field day tomorrow; they usually must go to the trailer court for their scandal."

"More power to them," she retorted. "I enjoy gossips. I don't mean that I enjoy gossiping, but that I can innocently give others reason to gossip. I enjoy knowing that they are clacking away their little tongues over something I've done —the more outrageous the better. Makes me feel good."

"And makes them seem smaller in your eyes. But if you'd really like to provide them with a spectacle, we can open the blinds and stage a performance."

"Such as what?" she asked with narrowed eyes. "No, thank you. I'm more interested in your library. *And* the artifacts. I want to see what the archeologists missed." Her stare was candid. "I want to see the youth dances."

"Do you now?" He pushed away from the table as if to get up. "You'll also want to see my etchings." Nash laughed at her sudden expression. "Honest, I do have etchings and you will want to see them. I have several plates on the Mycenaean Age, some early Minoan and late Egyptian sketches. I also have a few rare ones, old treasures, done by an artist attached to Napoleon's army. I think you'll enjoy them."

"Napoleon? In Egypt?"

"Was, yes." He closed his eyes for a moment in concentrated thought. "Near the end of the eighteenth century I think, following his Italian conquests. Somewhat like another man before him he was really seeking a trade route to India, but he wound up on the Nile with the army and the artist. Lasted a bit over a year; he and the artist lived to return home but the army wasn't lucky. The artist—by name of Denon, Vivant Denon—carried with him in his imagination and on paper some of the most peculiar treasures yet taken from Egypt."

"Peculiar?" she questioned.

"Wait until you see them. Highly prized by certain types of collectors, and rather expensive today."

"How did you get them?"

"There was a day when they were quite cheap—a dime a dozen. Time has increased their value of course."

"Very well, you've aroused my curiosity; I want to see these precious treasures."

"Rather thought you would." He stood up and pulled back the chair for her. "Leave the dishes for the maid."

"You have one?" she said quickly, more sharply than she had intended. His casual statement had caught her off guard.

"Me," he answered, "I can do them later." Her tone had drawn his curious, questioning scrutiny. "Meanwhile the night is young and you're so . . ."

Shirley turned, raised her lips. "Yes?"

"You're so hungry for knowledge." He pretended not to see the minute annoyance on her face. "Ten paces forward and turn right at the closed door."

He preceded her across the room and opened a door into another that she had not seen in her first tour of the house. Nash entered the darkened place and snapped on the lights. The door revealed a book-lined room, four solid walls of volumes reaching from ceiling to floor without a window opening anywhere, a room which contained nothing else other than two easy chairs, a single floor lamp placed between them, and a record player.

"Well!" she said with pleasant surprise.

"Conducive to thinking," he explained, "either deep or shallow depending upon the inclination, and a very nice place for dreaming I might add. A woolgatherer's paradise. There's no interference from the outside—the room is fairly soundproof. Try it sometime." He grinned at her and held it until she had responded. "The books are arranged in no particular system or order except by their general nature and my own habits. Starting there," he motioned to a far corner, "mathematics, philosophy, chemistry, biochemistry, geology and geography, down there, the psychology and sociology. Sociology extends around the corner and continues there. It seems to be on the increase, you see. Here, a bit of linguistics and much on astronomy. A favorite of mine, that—plus archeology and anthropology. Over there is paleontology, and those two shelves are devoted to physics." He studied the two shelves and added softly, "That, too, seems to be on the increase."

"No books?" she asked curiously while staring about the impressive room. "Just books for reading?"

"Fiction? These are more provocative and some are certainly wilder than fiction. But yes—some." He moved the guiding finger. "Over there."

"Not many," Shirley said a moment later.

"Not much time for it," he confessed.

"Pardon me," she contradicted, and then smiled to rob the contradiction of its sting, "but I know a man who thinks you have all the time in the world. To do nothing."

"The man would be shocked to discover how wrong he is!" Nash declared almost angrily. He regretted the words immediately, conscious of the effect they would have on her, aware of the implications and questions that would spring into her mind if not to her lips. His tone changed to a light banter as he sought to erase the impression that snapped reply might have given. "The man is jealous—he thinks I'm loafing and he wishes he could."

"Indeed?" she said dryly. Her steady glance on his face said columns more. And then she, too, changed her tone. "And now, sir, the etchings. Or am I being forward again?"

He brought them to her from some secure resting place in some other room of the house, returning to the book-lined room with both hands full. While he was away she had started the record player and now she sat in one of the two chairs, awaiting him. He placed the gentle burden in her lap and she held it there in preliminary examination. They were two large loose-leaf volumes like scrapbooks and many folders and folios, all bound or wrapped in a sturdy material for maximum protection. Before she looked at any of the pictures she saw that all were covered with a thin, tough, plastic-like cellophane to protect them from dirt and exposure; even so, some of the paper was yellowed and cracked with age and occasionally a jagged streak ran across the face of an illustration to betray its ancient brittleness. She saw all that and the lines of the drawing before she actually saw the intricate pictures themselves, before the careful detail stood out against the whole.

She even found herself searching for the name of the illustrator in the lower corners of the first picture, before the massed lines separated themselves and the individual figures commanded her attention. Her eyes wandered across the face of the page and stopped on a figure she recognized, Hathor, the Egyptian goddess of love. She looked to see what the goddess was doing and discovered the man at her side.

Shirley Hoffman heard a sharp indrawn breath and then realized it was her own. She glanced up quickly to see if Nash was watching, was laughing at her, but he had moved across the room. She looked back to the picture, really looked at it, and felt the warm blood rush to her face. The mounting flush angered and annoyed her and she strove to conquer it, to thrust it away. She concentrated on Hathor, and those other figures clustered about the goddess. Across the room the music played softly on.

She was not aware of the passage of time, nor of the room, nor consciously aware of one record after another dropping onto the turntable to play itself out. Occasionally she would glance up with a start, turn to look about her, to look for Nash. Sometimes he would be sitting in the chair behind her, concentrating on a book, or again he would be gone from the room altogether without her knowing that the door had opened or closed. She saw him once with a bottle of ale in his hand and next time she looked the bottle was missing, but still there was no thought of passing time. She vaguely realized the unwanted flush long had left her face, realized there was no longer that burning, creeping sensation beneath the skin of her cheeks. Instead, there was something else she couldn't immediately identify and it was not confined to her face. A hungry, yearning something that seemed akin to the ancient people who were but inked lines on paper, a something that seemed to search for an outlet still hidden in an undefined vacuum.

With each turned page, each carefully shielded drawing plucked out of a folder, examined in minute detail and then replaced for the next, she understood a little more of what had been meant by "peculiar treasure." She found herself contemplating the mind and personality of the men who had done these illustrations, wondering about their various receptions in the times in which they lived, speculating on what they had first found in those faraway lands to fire their imaginations in this manner. Had Napoleon himself seen this one, that one—and what had he thought of it? Near the end, she realized something else. The men who had done these things were not conventional thinkers, in the conventional sense. They too, by this evidence, did not think as she thought, as Dikty thought, or even Cummings. Did they think along other lines, in abstractions or symbols, or perhaps in a manner utterly foreign—as Nash did? Who was to say now? They were dead, buried, perhaps even their graves lost and forgotten. They could only be half judged by what they had left behind, and what present day human could judge evidence such as this with a mind free of bias and prejudice, free of smirking obscenities? A most undeserved obsequy.

She awoke to her surroundings. When she awoke she found her hands folded in her lap atop the stack of pictures, found the record player still turning on some nameless waltz. She concentrated on that, on the name of the piece, and when she had placed it, the full awareness of the room had returned to her. Without turning, she knew Nash was seated in the other chair behind her. He made no noise, did not move, but she knew he was there. She also knew she was hungry and what had caused it, and what could satisfy it.

Calmly, quite detached, she analyzed the hunger and traced it to its root. The vacuum was no longer undefined and the outlet no longer hidden from her searching mind.

Shirley Hoffman stood up, transferred the contents of her lap to the chair seat, and stepped around the floor lamp to stand behind the second chair. Nash was deep in a printed page. Eagerly, boldly, she bent over him and locked his un-suspecting head in her arms. Then she kissed him, held him locked there for a racing eternity, unwilling to break the contact of their lips.

He jumped when their lips met, struggled to break free but she only tightened her arms. Then she sat quite still. Had she been watching his hands she would have seen his fists clench in determination, only to open slowly in a pe-culiar surrender. Had she been watching his hands and had she been able to read the enigmatic messages there, she would have known that he was fighting an intangible, fighting to reject and not use the easy access she had provided into a very private place—the last remaining privacy man has in the world. The privacy of her mind, the very much hidden world of personal thought. As she persisted in the long kiss his hands unclenched, lay limp and open, and he walked through a doorway into a room without her knowing it. Gregg Hodgkins had required years to discover that entrance and the aftermath.

Shirley broke away, stepped back, breathing heavily.

Nash stared up at her in wild astonishment and uttered a single word. She did not know the word, it was not English and so was strange to her. But by the intensity with which he said it, she knew it to be an epithet.

"Are you angry?" she said after a moment.

His answer was not an answer to her question. It was something else altogether, but she thought he was referring to the kiss.

"So long!" Nash exclaimed, still astonished. "So incredibly long. I couldn't see the end at all."

Chapter 9

"You owe me so much," Shirley said unexpectedly, "so very, very much."

Nash was suddenly startled, wondering if he had made a major error in judgment. He remained on his knees before the fireplace, coaxing into life the small fire he had kindled to dispel the chill the night weather had brought. It would be hot again tomorrow, the summer stickiness of Knoxville, but tonight the mountains had sent down an unusual coolness that penetrated even the house. He did not turn to where she sat, did not pause in the casual act of fanning the newborn flames into steady life, but waited silently for the words that must follow.

She put down her coffee cup into its saucer. "You owe me an explanation. Many explanations."

He felt the disappointment welling up within him, the keen sense of error. "I do?"

She must have nodded behind him. "May flies," she said. "An unexplained search for an unexplained immortality. And why it was found too late to save a life. *What* was found too late? Oh, you owe me so very much!"

A dread, growing weight was suddenly lifted. Nash almost laughed aloud as he asked, "Who wants to know? You —or a man you know?"

"I do," she retorted promptly. "But I suppose the man will know, eventually. I rather like my job."

He turned slowly about and sat down, reached out a hand to pat the hearth rug beneath him. "Come here."

Shirley crossed the room and sank down beside him. "This is nice." She folded her legs beneath her skirt.

"Most of the ordinary things in the world are nice. Cling to them while you can."

"Am I going to hear a lecture?" she asked archly.

"No. Of course not."

"I was only teasing. Talk to me. About May flies."

"It may get awfully boring."

"Then I'll stop you. I know how."

"Yes," he agreed dryly, "you know how. And what you don't yet know you'll learn. You have a long time to learn."

"Three score and ten," she quoted the cliche.

He said nothing to that, wrapped in bemused thought. Behind them the growing flames crackled in the kindling, spreading warmth across their backs; before them the house was nearly dark and wholly quiet, the last record having run its course and all lights but one extinguished. The books and prints had been put away, and the door to the library closed when they were through with the room. Gilbert Nash speculated on the woman sitting beside him. It may have been a fantasy—pure imagination—but he wondered if he was entertaining his own granddaughter, *ever* so many times removed. Her life was incredibly long.

"May flies," she finally prompted.

"May flies," he repeated. "The eggs are laid in fresh water, to be scattered by the current, finally to come to rest wherever they may. The larvae often live for several years."

"I know that," she interrupted.

"Be quiet. The adult are the ones that concern us. Do you know how long the adults live? A few hours. Only a few hours—they must live a full lifetime in less than a day. That seems strange to us, incredibly strange and incredibly tragic, because *we* live three score and ten." He glanced briefly at the girl beside him. "Sometimes longer. But in the space of those few hours the insect must accomplish his mission, fulfill whatever duties have devolved upon him, and prepare the eggs for the following generation. And then, die of old age before sundown. Is he aware that only a few hours have passed?"

"Well . . . I don't know."

"He is not. If he is able to think about it at all, a lifetime is a lifetime. If he is able to think about it, measure it, compare it, then he would surely know he was being cheated by nature. But he is not able to do any of these things because he has no points of comparison, no yardstick to measure the span of his life against the spans of other living creatures around him. So, he lives his full lifetime until old age catches him. You do that, don't you?"

"Well, of course. But I'm not . . ."

"You aren't a fly. You are a human. A human has the means and the intelligence to think, to reason, to measure. Humans measure time in a variety of ways, have measured time required to make one journey around the sun and have called that a year. Therefore you know what a year is and how many of them you may reasonably expect before old age catches up with you. The insect cannot do that and must rely on instinct, must see to it that his work is done to beat that instinctive deadline. But insect and human are both following the same pattern: birth, life over a given span, death. The May fly is as old at the end of the day as you will be at the end of three score and ten. There is no real difference except that each lives according to a different measure of time."

"You're drawing an analogy."

He nodded. "An analogy. The insect lives his span and that is that. He doesn't know about you; if he did, he would be amazed, would be unable to believe that you could live for thousands of years—according to *his* timetable. But you know you aren't living for thousands of years because his timetable is but a few hours in your life. His timetable is below you, and insignificant. Very well then, what is above you? Is there a larger timetable on which *your* three score and ten are but a few hours as well?"

Shirley opened her mouth and then snapped it shut again, the sudden words unutterable as his startling suggesting penetrated. She was staring up into his face with fascination.

"You are aware of course that other living things on earth outlast your own lifetimes: elephants, parakeets, some species of fish, some of those remarkable trees on the Western Coast live for thousands of years. Each of them may have its own means of measuring the passage of time, but it certainly isn't by your standards and your timetables. Life spans, and the schedules by which those spans are measured may be either large or small, depending upon who is doing the measuring. You may live several thousand years longer than the insect; those trees may live several thousand years longer than you, relatively speaking. Do you think the trees represent the absolute limit?

"Hasn't it ever occurred to you that something else may live untold thousands of years beyond you, beyond the trees, may live a fantastic length of time according to your standards? But then, your standards aren't valid when applied to a different scale, a different concept of life. No more than the standards of the May fly would be if he attempted to fit you into his life concept. You look down upon the insect from your longer life span, to realize he is gone in a few of your hours. May not something else look down upon you, see you vanish in a few hours?"

"All this," Shirley said in a small voice, "is leading up to something. I can feel it."

"All this is leading up to Gilgamesh and his supposed immortality. I repeat, *supposed* immortality. An immortal according to common definition is a person who never dies, a person with unending existence. Gilgamesh was no immortal; he was only thought to be because he existed before the ancient poets were born and was still here after they had gone. He seemed immortal to them because he did not grow old and die as they did, because he did not follow their timetable to the grave. Therefore, it pleased them to build a host of spurious legends about him, around him, to make of him something he was not.

"The human species has a terrible blind spot: time. Because they are unable to reason and to measure, they reasoned time into existence and then measured it according to standards they could easily understand. But humans also have egos, and whenever and wherever possible, those egos are catered to; so they built time around themselves and used measures that fitted themselves alone. They cast the entire universe into their own time mold, judging it by their own vain standards as if those standards were the universal prime law. Humans believe they alone live *natural* life spans, the oft-mentioned three score and ten, while all else in creation is either above or below normal. Their vanity must make them the normal ones. They look down upon the insect as subnormal because he lives only hours or days of their time; they openly gape and marvel at those hoary old trees because the trees live an abnormal length of their time. They will never admit that the insect, or the tree, or something else altogether may know time in the true normal—if the true normal actually exists."

"Does it?" she asked.

"I wouldn't know. I'm not that big." He shook his head.

"Humans believe they are the pinpoint upon which all creation revolves."

"That doesn't sound fair."

"No, it doesn't. But I believe it to be the truth. An ego living on an island with millions of similar egos of the same pattern will eventually arrive at the erroneous conclusion that they, the egos, are creation and therefore all else must conform to their schedules and standards. Your histories are full of repetitions of that."

"But there is a way out?"

"Is, yes. Get kicked off the island by something bigger." Shirley was still watching his face. "Or have that bigger something move onto the island with them."

"Fine theory, but it doesn't prove out in practice. An individual ego here and there may be convinced but the greater mass will not. So—Gilgamesh. Those ancient ones could not see the contradiction in their own legends; they said he was an immortal, seeking the local equivalent of the fountain of youth. If he were immortal he wouldn't have need of the miraculous waters, but if he needed the waters he could not be an immortal. They confused cause and effect to build a contradictory legend."

The fire burned merrily behind them, warming their backs and sending fairy shadows dancing on the walls. High overhead in the night sky a heavy plane labored through the darkness, the noise of its motors trailing far behind it.

Shirley finally asked, "What *was* Gilgamesh seeking?"

"Water. Water to prolong his life."

"You said . . ." and she halted to remember his words. "You said he found it too late to save his life, he found his 'immortality' too late. What did you mean by that?"

"I meant that Gilgamesh sought water to live, and by the time he found it the die was already cast—and it was too late to save his life because he had gone too long without it."

"Water?" she asked incredulously.

"There was water on the island, the type of water natural to that island. But it was not his kind of water."

"I think you'd better explain that," she said dubiously.

"Suppose I tell you a story?"

"What kind of story?"

"About a shipwrecked mariner, a castaway." He stared at the moving shadows on the opposite wall. "About a man from another island who lived a part of his life span on the food and water natural to his island." He paused again. "About Gilgamesh."

"I want to know *all* about Gilgamesh."

"To satisfy a man you know?"

"To satisfy me."

"Gilgamesh was born on an island." He began slowly choosing his words with care. "An island that he thought was all the universe, all creation, until he left his childhood and began to learn that it was only an island, one among many. When he discovered there were many other islands and ships that traveled between them, he decided then and there he wanted to sail in those ships to visit the other islands, wanted to spend his life in such travel. As soon as he had left his childhood behind, he began the rigorous training necessary to become a mariner, began to accumulate the knowledge he needed to know to assist in the operation of those ships, began to learn about the other islands.

"And at the same time he learned about himself. He discovered—with quite a shock—that there weren't really many people on his island, not nearly as many as there were on other islands. In that one respect his island was really unique—the smallness of its population was a thing to be remarked. Eventually he discovered why, and the answer lay in genetics. The life in his world was one of lethal heredity because he, his parents, his relatives and his

friends were victims of doubled chromosomes, a quite
deadly trait that pared the newborn down to a minimum,
permitted only a fantastically low number of children to be
born with normal bodies. By far the majority of births were
stillborn, or mutated monsters that would not or could not
live. Perverse genetics in the form of an unbalanced number
of chromosomes was the curse upon the island and its people, and none there escaped it. Life very nearly became ex-
tinct, would have vanished altogether had not a saving
factor appeared in an attempt to balance the scale of nature.
Longevity. The only possible answer was an extended life
span so that the adults would have an opportunity to overcome the infant mortality rate, to prolong the race as a
whole.

"Very few infants lived. Those that did, lived a great
length of time, to enable them to procreate oftener and
longer, to enable them to keep the race alive until a few
more could be born to take their places. It was a poor balance, but the best that the tortured natural forces could
provide. So it was accepted. Gilgamesh accepted it as had
his parents before him, and accepted it because he found
himself with no *living* brothers and sisters, accepted it because he soon learned how thinly populated the world was.
But meanwhile he grew into early manhood, he completed
the training necessary to sail, and he married."

Shirley flashed him a startled look.

"He married early because it was the custom and the
means of prolonging the race. He married early because it
was required of him. Before he made his first voyage, he
had two children, both stillborn. And then he began a career
as a mariner, sailing between the islands.

"One of the things he quickly learned was that life—his
life—always hangs in the balance. The ships were the stout-
est, the best made, yet they sometimes ran afoul unseen
things that wrecked them. A ship could be hulled on any

voyage and when the ship went, life went with it unless a man was very lucky; the islands of safety were scattered amazingly far and wide, and only a few mariners managed to reach one when a ship was lost. Those few who saved themselves had another problem: the food and water found on an island might not always be compatible with life—his life. Food wasn't as serious a problem as water, because the water welling up on the island of his birth was not the same as water elsewhere. That difference was crucial.

"It was a peculiar kind of water, natural enough if one remained on the island during his lifetime, but really quite rare if one visited the other islands and discovered how unusual it was. It was a water with certain, special qualities not found in very many other places that the ships visited. Hence, those ships must carry huge stores of it to enable them to make complete round-trip voyages without refilling the tanks. The water of the other worlds was drinkable in emergencies—yes, but it was water of a drastically altered nature which failed to yield the mineral qualities necessary to sustain the lengthened life span. It was a poor substitute which, if one were forced to rely on it alone, would not sustain life the *natural* span. It was, in short, a thin liquid to prolong life a short while—nothing more. The natural water of the island on which one was born and raised was needed for a healthy life."

The girl had been sitting very quietly, listening to his voice and watching his profile against the flickering firelight. Now she said, "So Gilgamesh became a sailor. Despite the dangers to the mariner, despite the need for the peculiar water of his home world, he became a sailor. And he was shipwrecked."

Nash nodded somberly, his eyes still following the shadowy patterns on the far wall. "It was one of those dark unseen things that moved in a blacker sea, a hunk of rock that hurtled out of nowhere; it happened in an instant. He was with his wife—standing in their cabin engaged in idle conversation when the alarm bell rang. And in the next instant he was hurled through a breach in the cabin wall, not knowing if his wife had found time to prepare herself."

"Did he . . . did he ever find her?"

"Did, yes, when her body was found in a wrecked city."

Shirley closed her eyes, moved her lips to form the words, "I'm sorry," without actually speaking them. She said nothing aloud, waiting for him to continue.

"So Gilgamesh hunted water, the kind of water needed for his kind of life. He had his own emergency rations and he doled that out for a little at a time, sipping at it while he accustomed himself to the new, weaker water he found on the strange island. It did not last forever of course and was soon gone, but he continued his search all over the known world, over all the world that he could manage to cover, always hoping that somewhere he would find it. You see—it was quite inevitable that those ancient Mesopotamian poets should concoct stories about him, should make him out a demigod."

"But he *did* find it somewhere—too late."

"Did, yes. He never found it in its natural state, and so his body began to die—simply began to deteriorate for lack of it, the same as your body would deteriorate if you were deprived of water and forced to drink some other fluid. He was so long without it that when a near-substitute finally appeared in an artificial state, complete rejuvenation was impossible. Compare it if you like to the doctor who discovers a serum too late to heal his patient; the serum will prolong the patient's life a while, but nothing more."

"This water is manufac—oh!"

"Yes," Nash repeated dryly. "Oh."

"Heavy water?" she questioned.

"That's the popular name for it. Deuterium oxide. Eventually men began scientific experimentation for purposes of war, and produced heavy water."

"But that was only a short time ago. Thirty years ago," she protested.

"I told you Gilgamesh found it far too late to save his life."

She was silent for a long while and he said nothing to break the silence, allowing her the privacy of her thoughts. He sat with his back to the fire and listened to the quiet house, listened to the stillness of the night outside. Her nearness wafted the gentle perfume to his nostrils and he enjoyed that. Quite unconsciously she first straightened and then recrossed her legs beneath her skirt, briefly flashing slim ankles in the dim light. Shirley was silent for so long that at last he moved his head to look at her, to study the intense expression on her face. Their eyes met.

"All of this . . ." she paused and swallowed, "all of this is rather difficult to believe in one sitting. And not a little confusing."

"Is, yes. I'm aware of that," he smiled down at her. "I don't ask you to believe any of it, if you don't wish to." He moved his hand rapidly as though to wave it all away. "Consider it only a tale, told by another imaginative poet."

"No," she protested haltingly, "not quite that. I'm unable to grasp the whole thing, but not quite that. You'll have to forgive my slowness, but I'm only—human. It seems just a little too much to perceive and believe all at once."

"I understand."

"Once before," she continued slowly, fumbling with an idea difficult to translate into words, "I asked you how old Gilgamesh was—at the time of Noah, for instance. Oh, and by the way, I've discovered since that Gilgamesh predated the Biblical flood as well as postdated it, if we may believe the clay tablets. You see, I've been doing a little bit of research of my own."

"Good for you."

"But I'm curious about the age of Gilgamesh, about his original appearance on this—island. The tablets give no hint of course. How long ago was the shipwreck? How long ago was Gilgamesh washed ashore?"

Nash furrowed his brow. "Now *that* is difficult to answer. How would you mark time before the invention of the calendar? The best I can do is make an estimate based on the people and the life he first discovered on the island. And then compare those people to present-day anthropological studies."

"I'll accept that. Which people?"

"The Azilian culture."

"Azilian? I'm sorry, but that doesn't mean anything to me. I'm not familiar with it."

"It is generally identified with the early Mesolithic period in western Europe." He was still watching her face, watching for the shock that he knew would be there. "That roughly was 8000 B.C."

She sat still with her eyes closed.

"The climate was quite warm—very similiar to what it is today in that part of Europe; the last of the ice sheets had retreated northward and warm-weather animals were starting to appear. The people—the Azilians—were a small-statured but wild hunting race; they possessed half-tamed dogs to aid them in the hunt, and lived chiefly on the wild cattle and horses that roamed the countryside. A very fierce race. The Azilians later overran most of western Europe. I think: Spain, Switzerland, France, Belgium, part of Britain. Damned aggressive."

Shirley turned on him with wide staring eyes and he saw the reflected shock. "But that was nearly ten thousand years ago!"

He nodded agreement. "I think it was."

"Ten thousand years!" She groped for understanding. "I can't believe—but *when* was his wife found? Where was she?"

"She died in Lisbon, in 1755. An earthquake leveled the city."

Nash brought in from the kitchen a bubbling percolator and refilled their coffee cups, carrying hers across the room to place it beside her on the hearth rug. Kindling had been added to the waning fire, rebuilding its light and warmth. He indicated the coffee. "Dr. Nash prescribed."

"Thank you. I suppose I've been acting like a dope?"

"I wouldn't say that."

"I feel like one."

"Please don't."

"I try to keep an open mind," she explained. "I try to be at all times credulous and understanding and willing to learn new things. But sometimes I just can't help myself!"

"Quite human," Nash grinned. "Oh, quite human."

"That's just it," she still protested. "*Human.*"

"Stop it!" he said sharply. "I didn't mean it that way."

"I'm sorry." She lowered her eyes over the cup. After a moment, she said, "If you don't mind . . . I'd like to ask you something. And I promise not to make a scene."

"Fire away. I'll answer if I can."

"The shipwreck . . ." she began ". . . that shipwreck ten thousand years ago. You said that the body of his wife was recovered." She hesitated briefly as a quick, fleeting emotional shadow passed across his face. "Were there any other living survivors besides Gilgamesh?"

"Were, yes. The island was large and much of it was like an unexplored jungle. Movement was next to impossible where there were barriers but not means of transportation. Naturally, while he searched for water he also sought his companions who might have lived. He found a few of them, eventually. The rest had either perished with the ship or were marooned in some inaccessible place. Slowly, with time, those few survivors appeared."

"Are they . . . are they still . . . ?"

"Alive today? No. With one exception they met early death. Some died of injuries, some were old and could not exist on the water found here, some met with accidents. One deliberately committed suicide in a Roman arena."

Shirley questioned, "With one exception . . . ?"

Nash glanced at her curiously. "Do you have access to your government's wartime secrets? You can check this if you like. In France, in 1940, two scientists fled their country to avoid the approaching enemy; they took with them to England two hundred and ten quarts of heavy water—or to be more accurate, they left France with two hundred and ten quarts, barely a jump ahead of the invading Germans who wanted that treasure. The fugitives fled across the Channel with their deuterium oxide, which amounted to virtually the entire world's supply at that time and was therefore doubly precious. The two scientists arrived safely in England with one hundred and sixty-five quarts. But mark you this: They could not account for the shortage, could offer no reasonable explanation as to what had happened to the missing forty-five quarts. It was generally assumed they had been lost overboard."

"But they hadn't?" she queried.

He didn't answer her directly. "The loss of those forty-five quarts was the first clue to the existence of another survivor—a survivor who still lived at this late day." Again he turned to her, watching her eyes and her sensitive face, wondering if she was mentally following him. "A search was instituted for that other survivor, sparked by the very natural desire to be reunited. And finally a trace was found."

"Nothing more than a trace?"

"A trace. At Peenemunde."

Shirley frowned. "I should know that name."

"The German rocket site, where the V-2's were built."

"Oh—of course." Her frown had not quite vanished. "And a trace of him was found there?"

"A trace of her was found there," he corrected.

"*Her?* A woman!"

"A woman. It seems that she had been at Peenemunde for some years; since 1934, in fact, when the German government began seriously considering rocket experimentation. But now only a trace of her remained—she was gone, and forty-five quarts of heavy water had disappeared from the middle of the English Channel with her. It wasn't too difficult to guess why she had been at Peenemunde, why she finally left there, and where she was going next. Not when you knew the nature of the woman. After all this time she was still not reconciled to the world in which she now lived, still not willing to stay, *very* unwilling to accept an early death. She wanted a ship to return home." He paused.

Shirley absently shook her head, not speaking.

"When the Germans began rocket experimentation at Peenemunde she quite naturally gravitated there, pulled by a hope and a prayer stronger than herself. She was, frankly, impatiently awaiting the day when they would fumble and grope beyond mere war rockets, beyond rockets themselves, for she knew something better was needed to conquer space. Given time and the proper channeling of energies, the Germans would build a ship for her. But the Germans had neither time nor the inclination; they concentrated their product on the destruction of London and similar purposes of war.

"She then realized that Peenemunde was not the answer, that Germany would not last long enough to build the ship she desired. So she fled—and seized life-giving water as she did so. After Germany—what? What other nation was experimenting with rockets, what other nation was also experimenting with atomic energy—which also happened to be the true answer to space flight? She came to the United States. Once in the United States she very carefully surveyed the situation and assayed her chances. And then she made a choice. She married a young man who gave brilliant promise in the space project, aiding and abetting him by her own knowledge whenever possible, pushing here, thrusting him forward there, causing his name and work to appear in places and publications where it would be noted.

"The patient years of planning and scheming finally paid off and eventually her husband found himself working for the Ridgerunner Project, found himself at Oak Ridge, and probably much to his surprise, found himself assisting in the designing and building of an atomic reaction motor which was capable of hurling a ship through space. At last her long-awaited victory was within her grasp and it seemed only a short wait before she could sail again. Her husband, now useless and something of a dangerous weight about her neck, was murdered."

"Carolyn Hodgkins!" the girl exclaimed.

"Carolyn," he nodded. "She is determined to get off the earth and she will not be stopped as long as she lives." Nash fell silent listening again to the house and the night.

"Carolyn Hodgkins is a—a survivor?"

"Is, yes."

"The only other one? No more than—two?"

"No more than two."

"Is . . ." she hesitated with some embarrassment. "Is she the only one determined to live—and to leave?"

"She is. The other one long ago resigned himself to remaining here, a premature death. Without dramatics, without mock heroism, he simply accepted the situation and is now quite content to stay, to await what comes." Nash moved slightly on the hearth rug, turning and lifting a hand to touch her arm. "You must remember that the only thing I ever loved is buried here. I *want* to stay."

There was a minute sound somewhere in the night, and Nash lifted his eyes to stare through the window at the sky.

"I think I can understand that," Shirley said haltingly and still with evident embarrassment. "And I'd like to ask . . . Please, this is rather personal but . . ."

"Ask it." He was listening hard to the darkness.

"Did he—did you ever marry again?"

"Marry? No, not in that sense. I have—mated—many times, but I never married again."

"Were there, I mean are there, any descendants?"

"Yes, a few." He shook his head. "A very, very few. My genetic curse still follows me, always will. But there are a few."

Shirley looked up, saw his gaze on the window and followed it, uncomprehending. "The descendants would not know, of course. They couldn't know."

"They have no way of knowing. I suppose most of them are pleasantly surprised to find themselves living to an unusual age. Unusual in respect to those around them."

"Do you know any of them?" she persisted. "That is, do you *meet* them? I'm sorry I can't express that more clearly— I'm all jumbled up inside and my thinking isn't any too lucid. But in your—travels, have you ever found any of your own descendants?"

"Have, yes." He was grinning broadly at some inner secret as he climbed to his feet and then reached out to help her up. She was standing quite close to him and he rested his hands on her shoulders. "It's always a startling thing; they appear most unexpectedly and in the strangest places. Of course there is seldom an outward physical trait to mark them, so I've learned to look for the subtler things—

the attitude, the personality, the mental awareness and the matter of their longevity. That's the greatest clue, that and a talent for mental telepathy—for extrasensory perception." He shook her playfully. "Yes, it happens every now and then, Makes me feel something like a fatuous grandfather.

"You tell the man what you please, or omit what you please. I know the man's curiosity—and so I've not told you everything that I could." He hadn't told her, for instance, that a microphone had been planted in Dikty's office long before Dikty thought of putting an instrument in his. "I leave it up to your conscience, Shirley. Say as much or as little as you please. Only a word of warning for your own safety—consider first how much will be believed."

"That's my greatest problem," she admitted.

Shirley moved toward her purse on the table. "It's really late. I've got to go. And do you know what I'm going to do? I'm going to sleep on everything that you've told me—everything about sailors and shipwrecks and survivors—and tomorrow I'll decide whether or not to believe it myself."

"A wise decision, and let me know your answer. And in the meantime, thank you for the dinner. Practicing was fun."

She lifted her lips invitingly. "I liked it, too."

Nash kissed her briefly. "Tomorrow we can do it again."

"Tomorrow?" she questioned.

"*Some* tomorrow. You have several thousand coming."

Again she hesitated and lifted a forefinger to his lips. Changing her mind before the thought could be spoken, she repeated, "I've really got to go."

Nash pulled the car keys from his pocket and shook them in her face. "You'll either wait for me or you'll walk. And that's quite a distance to town." They were moving toward the door and he reached around her to snap on the outside light. He opened the door and stood aside for her.

"I'll wait for you—or I'd never get home. And I'll bet you that I'm late for work in the—*Gilbert!*" Shirley screamed his name and shrank back, blocking the doorway.

Chapter 10

THE LONG, raw sleepless night was reflected on her face. Hoffman sat miserably behind Dikty's desk in the inner office, struggling to keep her eyes open and holding up her head in both hands. Her head ached with a throbbing intensity and no amount of aspirin and strong coffee had been able to wash it away. Her legs were tired, tired from walking back and forth across the yard, from running in and out of Nash's house, and her body was as tired as her legs after a highly-keyed night of excitement and nightmare.

"Tell me again," Cummings demanded savagely, "again and again!" He grasped the desk with both hands and seemed ready to overturn it. "Where did he go?"

"I don't know! I've told you, I don't know." She held her head tightly, afraid it would burst from pain and the booming anger of his voice: "He just disappeared."

"Where?"

"I don't know."

"When?"

"I don't know. Before the police got there."

"Why did you call the police? Why didn't you call me?"

"Because he told me to. I didn't think of you—not then. Not until later."

"And later he was gone?"

"Yes."

"But you don't know when? You didn't see him go?"

"No—no, to both."

"You were together all evening? In the house?"

"Yes."

"Alone?"

"Yes."

"You didn't know Dikty was there, was tailing?"

"No. I hadn't seen Mr. Dikty all day."

"Where did you pick up Nash?"

"At the library. He invited me to dinner—or maybe I invited him. I can't remember now!"

"What happened after you left the library?"

"We walked along the street to his car and he drove me to his house."

"Nothing else? You didn't stop anywhere, do anything?"

"No—well, he did pause a moment. To look in a florist's window."

"To get some flowers?"

"No, it was closed."

"He just stood there looking at the window? Did he seem pensive—thinking about something?"

"Yes . . . he did. I had to speak to him two or three times to catch his attention. I suppose he was daydreaming or something. He gave me some flippant answer about not being able to buy a plant." She put the tips of her fingers to her closed eyelids, pressing inward in a vain effort to relieve the ache.

"And then he drove you out to the house? No stops?"

"No, no stops. I cooked dinner."

"What about after dinner? What happened then?"

"He showed me his library. He has a big room entirely lined with books, all manner of books."

"I saw that a few hours ago," Cummings snapped. "Then what?"

"We played records and I looked at the—the books."

The supervisor leaned low over the desk, thrusting his face within inches of hers. "You're lying! You didn't look at his books."

"Oh, all right then! I looked at some pictures."

"Pictures . . . ?"

"He has dozens of them. Old prints of Egyptian scenes, Babylonian scenes—everything."

Cummings drew back to study her. "Pictures," he repeated softly. "What was he doing all this time?"

"Reading. In the chair behind me."

"All the time? He never left the chair?"

"No. Yes, he did. Sometimes I would look up and he wouldn't be there."

"Gone from the room do you mean?"

"Yes," she answered miserably.

"How long was he gone?"

"I don't know. I'm afraid I didn't pay too much attention. The hours slipped by—sometimes he would be there, and sometimes not. I can't tell you how long he was gone."

Cummings grunted sourly. "Gone. Nobody knows how long, nobody knows where."

"I couldn't help it, I tell you! I was lost in what I was doing. An army could have marched through the room."

"Pictures," he said once more, skeptically. "All right, after the pictures, what?"

"He went into the kitchen, made coffee. He built a fire in the fireplace. And then we sat there and talked."

"What about?"

"History—I mean prehistory. All about Gilgamesh, and Noah, and the ice age, and the Azilians—"

"What's that?"

"Prehistoric men who lived in Europe. Thousands of years ago."

"Just talking? All that time?"

"Just talking, until I realized how late it was. He was going to drive me back to town."

"And then?"

"And then he opened the door and I saw . . . I saw . . ."

Glaring memories of the beginning of the nightmare rushed to the front of her mind, created a prickling sensation along the skin of her arms. She tried and failed to express a chilling shudder. "Mr. Dikty—dead."

"What did Nash do?"

"He ran down the steps, turned him over."

"Did you see the lipstick?"

"No, not then. Some policeman pointed it out later."

"You don't know if the lipstick was there when Nash turned the body over?"

"No. All I could see . . . was . . ."

"Did you ever see Dikty with another woman? Someone who was not his wife?"

"No. I never did. He wasn't that kind of man."

"*Some* woman smeared lipstick on his mouth," Cummings said bitterly. "And *somebody* strangled him."

Hoffman didn't bother to answer. Her head had sunk nearly to the desk top.

"All right," Cummings said desperately, "let's go back to where we started. What happened after he turned the body over?"

"I only stood there, looking at it. And he said something I couldn't understand. Something strange."

"In a foreign language, do you mean? What did it sound like—German? French? Spanish?"

"No, none of those. It didn't sound like anything I'd heard before. He said two or three words—angry words." She briefly raised her head to stare at the supervisor. "I could tell he was angry, terribly angry."

"So am I," Cummings snapped at her. "You have no idea—yet—just how angry I am! I'm going to have somebody's life for this. What next? What did he do?"

"He said to me, 'did you know Dikty was here?' and I told him, I didn't."

"Did he believe you?"

"Yes."

"You were never aware that Dikty had been tailing either of you?"

"No, I never knew it."

"And then what?"

"He put his fingers—his hand, I guess, inside Mr. Dikty's coat a moment, and said he was dead. And then he bent down closer to look at his face. Mr. Dikty's face was . . ."

"Black," Cummings supplied. "Hadn't you ever seen a man strangled to death before?"

"Never," she paused. "I think I was sick."

"What did Nash do?"

"He told me to go back in the house and call the police."

"And you did. Without calling me first."

"Yes. I didn't think of you, then." She rubbed her hands across her face. "After I called the police I sat down. I think I went to the bathroom; I must have been upset. Everything was so—so mad and whirling."

"What did Nash do?"

"I don't know. I don't remember seeing him again."

"You stayed in the house until the police arrived? In the chair?"

Hoffman nodded. "There, or in the bathroom."

"And the police gave you the works." He glanced at her briefly, studied the top of her head. "You can't really blame them; you were found alone with the body and you weren't wearing much lipstick. They like to leap to hasty conclusions."

"I didn't put any more on," she told him desperately. "We weren't going anywhere. He was driving me home and I was going to bed. I didn't bother to make up."

"I apologize for that," he said suddenly, softly. "I can imagine how you felt in jail. If the dumb bastards had bothered to compare your lipstick to that smeared on the body, they'd have seen the difference. I apologize, Hoffman. And they'll sweat for it."

She dropped her head to the desk. "Oh, don't bother."

Cummings perched on the edge of the desk and draped an arm across her shoulder. "Think a bit, now. While the two of you were sitting there talking— Did you hear anything? A noise?"

"No, I didn't."

"Did he?"

"He might have. He seemed to be listening and looking at the window. I didn't pay any attention to it at the time. But he might have heard something."

"He didn't investigate it?"

"No. We didn't sit there much longer. Just a few minutes more. And then I got ready to leave."

"At any time during the conversation, during the evening, did he mention going away? Leaving town?"

"No, it never came up."

"Did you make plans to meet again?"

Her head moved in a subdued nod. "I was going to see him again today. No definite plan, or place. But I told him I'd see him."

"He agreed?"

"Yes."

"Do you think he'll still keep that date?"

"I don't know. I haven't had time to think about it. He

said—oh!" She jerked upright, startled. "You'll arrest him! If he comes to see me, you'll arrest him."

"Of course, I can't think of better bait!"

"But that isn't fair!"

Cummings got up from the desk, stood off to look at her. "Which side are you on?"

She glared at him for a bewildered moment and suddenly burst into tears.

"Stop that!" he commanded. "I can't stand that."

She only dropped her head to the desk and continued crying. Cummings hovered over her for an indecisive moment, unable to do anything. Fretfully then, he paced a circle about the room and avoided looking at her. When he could no longer endure the sound of it, he stalked into the outer office, pulling the connecting door shut behind him. Out there, the crying was no more than a low muffled noise. He sat down heavily behind the girl's desk and put his feet up on the edge, and ran a nervous hand through his thinning hair. Placing the tops of his index fingers together above the ridge of his nose, Cummings stared past them and contemplated the doorknob.

What the hell—Dikty dead!

It wasn't Nash, damn that man! It wasn't Nash, despite the several minutes he'd been absent from the room where Shirley Hoffman waited, despite the fact that the murder occurred only a few feet from his front door. No. It wasn't Nash. It was a woman, a woman who had first kissed and then strangled Dikty to death. Kissed him by God! And then killed him while he lay in wait outside the door. Discovered him there on station.

What woman?

There was only one woman involved in this grisly business: Hodgkins's widow. (A woman who undoubtedly *made* herself a widow!) First Hodgkins, and then Dikty—but why? What the hell for? What could she gain? Had it been Hodgkins alone in the absence of the other factors, he'd be inclined to write it off as an insurance murder—but not this, not two of them. What in the devil's name did Hodgkins and Dikty have in common?

But that was simple, so simple that Hoffman could put it together; the one was a government scientist and the other was a watchdog over the scientist—the guarded and the guardian. A woman without a documented past had murdered both of them.

And there was Nash, also without a satisfactory past. But the one seemed to be *pro,* and the other *con.*

What kind of sense did *that* make when they were so obviously alike, when they seemed to be two peas from the same pod? Both of them physically similar, both without duly recorded and stamped beginnings in space and time, and most likely both of them in the country illegally. They were strangers—as though they had dropped down from the moon. He couldn't just bob up in Florida without a respectable, documented background—yet he had. She couldn't simply appear in upper New York state without a prior history of some sort—but she had.

Cummings felt a vague, disturbed notion that he was caught up in something not of his own doing, caught in something he couldn't comprehend or understand.

He abruptly left Hoffman's desk and went to the door, opening it slightly to look in on her. The tears had ceased.

"Hoffman . . . ?"

She raised her head. "Yes?"

"Think hard, now. Did you see any of the signs of a woman out there at the house? Anything at all?"

The girl turned and stared. "Why no!"

"Nothing at all? The bedroom? Bathroom? Something that I would have overlooked but you'd have caught?"

Wide-eyed she returned his gaze and shook her head. "Not a thing. I would have noticed."

Cummings sighed with defeat. "All right. It was just an idea. I sort of hoped—"

"I wouldn't have stayed a minute if I had seen something there."

"Okay, okay, forget it." He studied her worn face. "You'd better go home and get some sleep; you're not worth a plugged nickel to me the way you are now."

"I'm beat," she confessed. "Really beat. That was horrible!"

"I can believe it." His gaze lingered on her face and a trace of sympathy crept into his voice. "Get a cab and go on home. Shoo."

She came around the desk to lay a hesitant hand on his arm. "Mr. Cummings, I'm sorry I failed you. I've let you down terribly. I had built such dreams . . . When you told me I could work on the case with you, told me to call Mr. Dikty my cousin if trouble should come—well—I'm afraid I built such foolish dreams. I thought I would set the world on fire; I saw myself in all manner of pseudoheroic guises. I know better now."

Cummings lifted her drooping chin and smiled at her dulled eyes, haggard face. "A night in jail can kill the dreams in anyone. It's rough. Let the words wait until you've slept, slept around the clock. We can discuss these things tomorrow."

"Tomorrow," she repeated wanly. "He said that."

"He said what?"

"That I could cook dinner for him again tomorrow. He didn't mean today, but tomorrow. Any tomorrow. He said I would have a thousand of them."

"What did he mean by that?"

"I don't really know."

"All right. Go on home now and sleep. Go on."

Shirley Hoffman walked out of the office.

Cummings absently searched for the old familiar splotch

of sunlight on the scarred floor and listened to the girl's re-treating footsteps in the corridor. When she had gone he sat down rather heavily on a corner of the desk and picked up the phone, twirling a number on the dial by long and easy habit. Silent minutes fled by while a distant bell pealed and a puddle of sunlight slyly touched the tip of his shoe. An instrument at some far end was lifted from its cradle.

"Grove?" he asked the phone. "This is Cummings, in Knoxville. Can you send me two men on the afternoon plane? Good. Yes, they'll do. I've got a pair of suspects here and they've got to be found soon. And Grove, send about twenty-five thousand in cash with them. I want to take care of Dikty's widow. What? Yes—Dikty. Last night. Pass the news along to the boss. Okay?"

He hung up to thoughtfully study the pool of sunlight. After a moment he pulled the phone toward him and dialed the same number.

"Grove? Cummings again. Can you send out a new office girl on the same plane? This one is a dead loss; we'll have to replace her."

Cummings contemplated the sun on his shoes.

Chapter 11

COME OUT IN THE OPEN, Carolyn—you're hiding in there somewhere.

Somewhere among that tangled maze of lights and crazy intersected streets, somewhere in that up and down sprawling city spread over many hills and valleys, somewhere in that jumble of buildings large and small, somewhere in that soft illuminated night below—you're hiding now. Or were, until an hour ago.

Nash perched on the hillside surveying the lights of the sleeping city spread out beneath him. By turning his head slightly he could see the dark outline of the road snaking out from the city, could see the smaller cluster of madly bobbing lights that were the police about his house. The police were down there now, with the strangled body of Dikty, with the near-hysterical girl. But back in the other direction the street lights of the city claimed his attention. He crouched in the underbrush on the side of the hill, studying the city and its lights.

Carolyn was in there—somewhere.

She was secreted there, safely hidden away from the prying eyes of the police, from Cummings, from himself. And *that* rankled. Secreted from him, the only one of all the billions of people in the world who actually knew her, had known her a long, long time. She had been hidden away—somewhere—since that day many weeks ago when she first deserted and then murdered her husband—the last in a line of many such husbands. Hidden so well that none had ever found her. The police, then Cummings and Dikty, then he himself had followed every suggestive trail, had searched out the hotels, the rental units, the real estate agencies, the very utility offices that must supply her with those things she wanted and needed: water, electricity, gas. But she had not been found.

There was no evidence that she had slipped out of town and, until tonight, none that she had stayed. No house, apartment or room could be located that might have been rented to her, no automobile had been sold to her, the family bank account had remained untouched. Knowing Carolyn, he knew those items meant nothing in themselves—the woman who now called herself Carolyn Hodgkins had had ample time to accumulate and hide material wealth in any part of the world. Carolyn Hodgkins could have existed without beauty parlors these past few weeks, without entertainment, without small luxuries, without clothes, without this or that to which she had become accustomed in her lifetime. But she could not exist without food and water and it was highly unlikely that she had existed without electricity and possibly gas. Still, there appeared no record or evidence that those things had been furnished her. Any reasonable man examining the known facts would finally conclude the woman was no longer on the scene.

But she still *was*. The second death proved that.

She had killed again with a swift and sure purpose. It was not an idle killing because the man happened to be standing there watching the house. She had kissed him to suck his mind of information, and then she had killed him. Carolyn had remained on the scene all these past weeks while the search continued. It was she who had been following him as he followed the plodding Dikty; she whose eyes had bored into the back of his skull with malevolent intensity. She had been following Dikty, and Nash had fallen into line between. Then Dikty must have been close to her, dangerously close.

Nash hugged the overgrown hillside, squinting into the darkness. Dikty *had* discovered her hiding place. And paid with his life.

She, who was currently known as Carolyn Hodgkins was imaginative, brilliant in her field—and cruel. Like those few other survivors she had come plummeting down from the wrecked vessel so many centuries ago, down into a tangled jungle of a land peopled with aborigines. That much he knew about Carolyn, although he had not seen her for ten thousand years, not since before the wreck. He remembered the woman as one of the navigation crew; possibly he had encountered her almost daily on shipboard, eaten in the same room or at the same table without paying attention to her. He knew her well enough, but like himself, she had been but one among a crew of nearly three hundred. He knew she was keen in navigation; given a ship and the power, she was quite capable of charting a route to any point in creation. The stars had changed their courses in ten thousand years, but not enough to prevent Carolyn from finding her way home again. He remembered Carolyn, remembered her from the voyage of ten thousand years ago—and he had since heard more.

It was difficult *not* to be talked about.

Old Raul had first told him something of her; Raul, who had fallen into the fertile, half barbaric country surrounding the Nile and in pure self-preservation set himself up in the priesthood. Raul had once crossed the Mediterranean in his declining days, seeking a substance of truth to the

Gilgamesh legends, and had told him a little about a third survivor. A third who lived far to the south, deep in the southern regions of the African continent; for more than a hundred years the continual rumors and stories drifted north on the lips of slaves, in the campfire tales of traders and thieves roaming the land. A woman, a beautiful white woman in the jungle fastness, a fiery, golden goddess who had fallen from the skies and had been enthroned by the warriors. She was brilliant; she was imaginative; she was cruel. She gave lands and crops and wealth and wives to those who served her; gave sudden death to those who did not. She introduced the rites and rituals of human sacrifice, taught the art of bow-making, of honing better spears and blades, taught a rudimentary knowledge of the heavens which rapidly degenerated into a mystical religion. The white goddess seemed to live forever.

They could not guess which of the ship's crew she might be, old Raul and he, but by analyzing her conduct they narrowed the probable suspects to a handful. And later, much, much later, when the means of transportation were available, he had gone searching for her only to find the goddess and the warrior race so much vanished dust.

She had come to his attention again in his own land, his own yard, when the ritualistic dances of bulls and youths appeared in the Aegean Islands. He *knew* the original source of those rites, knew the faraway world among the stars where such dances were a common thing. It was an easy realization to know that only a survivor from the ship could have introduced an otherworldly custom into the Aegean lands. But he could not find her. He discovered long afterward that she was the lion-goddess personified on Cretan coins and rings, but the discovery came too late to assist him in his search.

And oddly enough, a brazen caricature of her existed on one of those illustrations brought back from Egypt by Napoleon's free-wheeling artist. A caricature copied from some other unknown source, but roughly recognizable. In time, he knew the identity of the white African goddess, the introducer of human sacrifice and cattle rites, but not once in all the ten thousand years had he managed to meet up with her. He was very close to her at Peenemunde, but once again she had slipped away. He was closer now, closer than he had been at any time since the ship met its death in space. He knew she was in the United States when he landed on the shore, knew what her destination would be once the destination itself had come into existence.

And so he had slowly drifted into Oak Ridge and settled down to await her appearance. And then one day a bewildered husband had come to him for consultation. And Carolyn was pegged.

She was not content to stay here, to spend her remaining though shortened years on a paradise planet. She yearned mightily to return home, to her native world where she might yet outwit death. Carolyn was younger than he, Nash reflected. Younger, less mature, more impulsive and certainly more hopeful. As well as more deadly. She had quickly enough shed the civilized conduct of her own world when adapting herself to this new one. Old Raul, Raul of the fabulous age and equally fabulous memory, had said that no one of their race deliberately brought death to another. No one until Carolyn found herself a despotic goddess, that was. Their struggling race was far too dependent upon life.

But Carolyn murdered her latest husband—and was pegged.

And then she killed the one man who had found out her hiding place. Why had she first kissed him? To discover if he held any knowledge not yet known to her, to discover if he knew the date and the place that one important ship would be hurled into the sky. Dikty might have known that, considering his occupation, his organization. Or he might have known nothing at all about it. Still, she could not afford to pass up the opportunity; and so she kissed and killed.

Dikty, of all men, had found her hiding place.

You're down there, Carolyn, down there somewhere in the maze of lighted streets or surrounding patches of darkness. But *where*, damn you, where?

Nash turned his head again, turned back to the black ribbon of road that wound out of the city and past his house. The tiny lights were still there, running crazily back and forth, in and out of the house and across the yard, running from the massed automobiles to the glob of light which illuminated the front steps and the strangled body.

Hoffman was due for some rough handling. He hoped she had the quick wit to telephone Cummings; he hadn't thought to tell her that before he left, hadn't thought to have her call her supervisor before she phoned the police. And he had left in a hurry before anyone could arrive, so there was no returning to give safe advice. She would have to take her chances, and perhaps Cummings could get to her before too long. He felt proud of the girl, quite proud. It was fatuously pleasing to discover some of his own character traits recurring in her, and he wondered briefly how long it might be before she guessed the truth?

When she had surprised him with that hot, rapturous kiss in his library, it had startled him not to perceive the end of her life.

But Carolyn had foreseen her husband's end, whether or not at that time she knew *she* would be responsible for his death. In the years of their marriage and the steady meeting of connubial love, she had known everything of her husband; had known his past before they had met, had known his present even though he attempted to leave his work at the laboratory, and had finally known his future—a short, surprising future that ended not too far away. In such close, personal meeting nothing is hidden from the one mind prying into another, nothing can remain secreted away in the mental nooks of the past, the open surface channels of the present or the unformed and gray vista of the future. The past is there, for searching; the present is there for reading; and the future is there for possible interpretation. Carolyn had finally looked into her husband's mind and found that its future path came to an abrupt halt. She must have attempted to search forward in his subconsciousness, to search for what was to come—and discovered only blankness, a blankness that meant the mind would shortly cease to exist. Hodgkins was going to die. Carolyn hastily deserted him.

But three weeks later she returned to murder him—why? To seal his lips? Knowing him as she did, she realized he might talk about her, about them, but not dangerously or wildly, for Hodgkins would be greatly concerned with his own sanity and would take pains to reveal no damaging facts which might lay himself open to suspicion, to self-injury. So at first she had not worried about the possibility of his talking, and had left him to wait out the weeks until his death—even perhaps wondering all the while how that death would come about. Hodgkins had then done the one thing which upset her calculations; he had called on Nash. If she had been keeping an eye on her husband, at all, she would have known of the visit and guessed at its conclusions. It was then likely that she had returned to their home that evening and perhaps for the first time realized that *she* was the instrument of death.

Hodgkins, being Hodgkins, would have blurted out all the details of the interview with the private investigator when his wife confronted him. *And* quite possibly have remarked the strange similarity between his wife and Nash. If Carolyn had not previously known Nash was in Knoxville, that would have been a startling shock. In an instant, she would have grasped all that his presence meant. Exit, Gregg Hodgkins. Nash would get no more information from him!

But it was such a useless death.

Nash had all the information he really needed to know —except one piece, of course, which did not develop until afterward. *Where was Carolyn hiding?* How had Dikty found that hiding place where all others had failed? What one morsel of evidence did Dikty have that the others did not possess or what shrewd deduction had he made that the others could not yet grasp? Or (ironically) what bit of dumb luck had he stumbled over which was not likely to be repeated for any who followed after?

Nash waited on the darkened hillside, crouching low and waiting for the anonymity of night to return to the road, to the house and the couple of acres. In memory he retraced the patternless path he and Dikty had strewn along the afternoon streets, retraced the seemingly aimless wanderings from one door to another, seeking a clue to Carolyn. The path that had actually led back to Carolyn in some dubious manner.

Below him on the road some few lights winked out and two or three automobiles moved off toward the city. There were still figures ranging about his house and even a lone flashlight poking among the trees of the apple orchard. He could not go back there, not now, maybe never. Someone would be staked out there until eternity, waiting for him to come back to claim his possessions. Cummings would regard that as mere routine; Cummings might even play it smart and send Hoffman in as bait.

Nash dropped his eyes from the distant scene, to stare at the looming, indistinct whiteness of his hands before him. Shirley Hoffman: *good-bye* probably, or at the very least, *so long*. To go back to her now for whatever reason would place her in a position of jeopardy, would force her to choose between him and her sworn loyalties. He did not want to force such a decision upon her. Still, he fervently hoped their paths might cross again someday, somewhere in the future. He would deem it a stroke of rare fortune to meet that girl again during her long lifetime.

In the first false light of dawn, Nash quit his position on the hill and sought out the poorly graveled road that circled and snaked around it. Fifteen minutes' slow, careful walking brought him to the steep ravine where he had ditched his car. He looked down at it with a tinge of regret, but it was not to be helped because every police officer in the state would already be searching for that car. Sometime in the next few days a rural traveler along the road would find it, report it, and it would be known that he was afoot. Nash turned his back on the smashed car and descended the rugged hillside.

He went with the wry memory of the hundreds or perhaps thousands of times he had done the same thing in the past, always felling something or someone.

The very first time had been his wild, surprised flight from the runty, fierce warriors who hunted with half-tamed dogs; they had been seeking wild boar and flushed him instead. The track of a flint spear across his arm had been the first wound he had known, had been the first realization that not all worlds and all people worshiped life as his own did. But the Azilian hunters had been a warning of what was to come. They were the last of the hunting races, but not the last of murderous mind.

He had attempted—with a fair success—to introduce some few civilizing measures to a wandering Neolithic people. He taught them to build wooden huts, to cast pottery, to breed work animals in captivity, to plant crops and work the soil, and to grind and polish tools. But in the end he again was forced to flee. He lived too long. They were not burdened with the superstitions to make of him a god or a devil, not imaginative enough to weave a legend of immortality—they were simply suspicious and decided he was evil. He ran for his life, and not for the second time.

He had drifted south to discover that the stone age in which he had found himself did not cover all portions of the planet simultaneously. Whereas a people or a tribe behind him worked laboriously with crude stone tools, ahead of him to the south, on all shores of the great inland sea, were new people who already knew the art of writing, knew the use of iron, of copper and bronze. Settling among them he had made another pleasant, surprising discovery—their art of writing was not of their own invention; it was a writing he could decipher and read with some difficulty. Some other unknown survivor of the wreck had been there ahead of him. That other man or woman could not now be found, but what he had left for Nash to find in later centuries was a warming thing.

In all those ten thousand years of cultural evolution—Azilian, Tardenosian, Maglemosean, the Campignian, Ertebblle, Asturian, (as men now named them), the later Egyptian, Crete, Minoan—in all those ten thousand years he had been forced to run from something—sometime—as he was running now, from men who believed he posed a threat to their national security.

The boy's sudden voice startled him.

"Hey there—where ya' going?"

Nash looked up, discovered the boy just across a fence. The lad was plodding along behind a small herd of cattle, and had twisted around to stare at Nash in his hasty descent of the hill.

"Hello," Nash called back. "I didn't see you. Going down to find a garage. My car's in the ditch up there." He pointed a vague thumb behind him.

"Where?" the boy asked curiously.

"You know that gravel road—the one that looks like a

corkscrew? Near a lot of pink-and-black rocks. I'm in the ditch up to there."

"Sure. I know that place. You didn't get hurt?"

"No. I'm all right. Just taking a short cut down into town."

"There ain't no short cut that way," the boy declared.

"No?" Nash paused to inspect the terrain, hoping the youngster wouldn't mention this incident to his parents. "Do you know a better one?"

"Sure," the lad replied with positive superiority. "Just climb over the fence and cut across here and go down there by them trees"—he turned to point out the grove—"and you'll see a path. Then just foller that around by the Norwood place—look out for his dogs, though. And pretty soon you'll come out right behind that trailer court down there. They got a phone."

"I'll do that, and many thanks."

"Be sure to watch out for the dogs, now."

"Will do. And thanks again." Nash climbed the fence and struck out across the pasture. He was among the shelter of the trees before the deeper significance of the boy's statement smote him. The trailer court had a phone.

It also had electricity, running water, sewage disposal, and canned gas if the trailer owner required it; and there were only simple connections to be made, all without the necessity of signing up for services at utility office in town. The court was quite removed and separated from the city, a village to itself; the rental of spaces was a weekly, monthly, or annual affair and settled on the spot with the proprietor. Anyone occupying a trailer in the fore of that court could—if she wished—simply glance out of the window to observe traffic along the road. Anyone having a particular interest in another person living higher up that same road could—if she wished—simply watch that person coming and going, all without the risk of being seen herself. No risk.

There, Carolyn? Living in a trailer?

Nash moved more swiftly along the downward path, threading his way among the trees and into the open country beyond them. A house loomed up finally in the growing dawn and he kept a cautious watch for dogs; one inside the house commenced a furious barking but no one interfered with his quick passage. He continued along the faint trail, sometimes losing it in the underbrush and then having to beat around in hasty circles to find it again. The boy had said "pretty soon" but nearly twenty minutes had passed and the sun was breaking the horizon before he sighted the trailer court. Nash stopped on the hill to study the layout.

It was modern, and of good size, having crushed rock for streets and individual walks up to each trailer door. Two sides of the court, those sides facing away from the town and toward the outlying hills, were lined with head-high shrubbery and young trees; the third side lay open, looking down upon the city, while the remaining boundary faced the road. Nash sat down with his back to a tree, watching the camp and studying the trailers.

They were of varying sizes and all conditions of age or newness; there was no hint in that. Several, this early in the morning, had wash hanging on the outside lines and he eliminated them from his search. A few children emerged from some, or men who clambered into nearby cars and drove off toward the city, or women who stood and gossiped with still other women in neighboring doorways. Still he stayed on the hill, patiently waiting and checking off the possibilities, one by one. Here, a couple appeared, to talk with wildly waving arms and then return inside; there, a baby was brought out into the warm sun, and then another. An old man came out, to walk around his home checking the air pressure of the tires. A grocer's delivery truck turned in from the road and made its slow way toward one of the units. Nash leaned forward with intent eyes, following its passage. The truck turned about, backed a few feet and the driver jumped out to open the rear door. A woman appeared from the nearby trailer to watch the driver. Nash relaxed against the tree, checking off that unit from his mental list.

By midmorning, he was down to a half dozen lifeless trailers, a half dozen which hadn't as yet given forth any sign of life or movement.

At noon, one of the half dozen was eliminated. A man opened the door, came out into the sun to stretch and rub the sleep from his eyes. That left five. In midafternoon the five remained and Nash was stretched out on his back by the ground, tired by the long watch and growing more hungry by each passing hour. In the late afternoon the morning exodus returned, the men who drove in from town, the children who had been playing about all day and those who'd been absent, the sons and husbands and fathers and paramours back from work for a night's sleep or play. One by one they arrived and Nash checked them into the trailers they had left that morning—with their coming two of the question marks were eliminated. A couple drove into the court and unlocked the door of one of those lifeless units; being followed shortly by a man alone who entered another. Nash supposed those three had left in the early morning hours before he assumed his watch.

Three trailers remained, three mute question marks. Two parked near the shrub-lined boundary before him and a third nearer the road.

It was dark.

Tired, legs cramped and stomach demanding food, Nash arose from the ground and moved slowly down the hill. The night around him was filled with tiny cricket noises and somewhere near at hand a bird was calling. A brick building set against the rear shrub line housed a public bath, and

Nash stopped there first for water, after working his way through the trees and shrubbery. The water helped a bit but still his hunger clamored for attention.

Nash left the building and edged toward the nearer trailer that claimed his interest. All about him were the human noises of the court, the odors of food and tobacco drifting on the heavy air, the sound of running water and noisy radios. Footsteps crunched on the loose rock as someone made his way to the bath building, and Nash faded back into the surrounding darkness until he passed.

The first of the three silent trailers came beneath his questioning fingers, still faintly warm from the day's hot sun. It was a long, low streamlined vehicle, sparkling silver and maroon when seen by daylight. His fingers had contacted one rounded corner of it and now he slowly edged toward the door, listening intently for sounds within. At a window he stopped, twisted his face up to read a notice pasted there. *For Sale*. Nash hesitated only a moment more and then boldly stepped to the door and tried the knob. It turned easily and the panel swung open on emptiness.

Within fleet seconds he was beside the second one. Using the same cautious approach as before, Nash worked his way around to the trailer door and tapped lightly. There was no answer. He tapped again and at the same time gently twisted the knob. The door was locked. Nash swung back into the concealing shrubbery and made his way toward the third and last trailer—that one nearest the road.

It too was silent—as dark, as seemingly lifeless as it had been all the long day. There was no movement from within, no sound. Nash knew the silent darkness of it was a lie. The door of the trailer stood open as if to welcome him and only a light screen door protected the interior from night-flying insects. Despite the absence of sound or motions the stillness was a lie, for there was the tempting odor of food. He lifted his nostrils to the odor, moved a single step nearer the screen. Abruptly there came a hissing sound and before he could jerk away there was still another—that of a suddenly bubbling percolator. Within a moment the odor of the steaming coffee was carried through the screen to him.

Nash grinned tightly and stepped to the screen door; he could see nothing at all in the blackened interior.

He said, "I've come, Carolyn."

Her answer came promptly, a low, husky, feminine voice from the trailer's interior. "I've been waiting for you, Gilbert. Waiting all day."

Nash nodded, still with the tight, knowing grin on his lips. "All day." The sound of her voice wiped out the millenniums as though they had never been. "All day."

"I discovered you up there watching me. You have the patience of a mule, Gilbert. And the intelligence."

He reached for the screen door.

Chapter 12

"CLOSE THE DOOR and turn on the lights," the husky voice said. "I want to look at you, old mule."

Nash gently pushed the door shut behind him and slid his fingers along the wall until he found the light switch. The sudden brightness made him squint.

"Oh, put away the gun, Carolyn."

She sat casually relaxed, confidently smiling, on a long divan that stretched across the front of the trailer, filling the space from wall to wall. She was dressed in light green lounging pajamas which seemed to caress her body, revealing the properly delightful curves here and there that made an enticing whole. No one would deny Carolyn was an attractive woman. The gun in her hand was the only jarring note.

She said, "I'll keep it, mule."

Gilbert Nash simply stood and looked at her, looked at the flowing crown of golden hair which now appeared somewhat lighter than he remembered; looked at the brilliant yellow eyes which had lost none of their fiery magnetism; looked at her body filling out the pajamas in bountiful fashion. The smooth skin of her face was—if one knew what to search for—only now beginning to show telltale signs of age, only now hinting at tiny wrinkles and indentations to come, and he thought the skin of her body would be as healthy. He looked at her hands—ignoring the gun in one of them—and thought he saw age; he looked at the deep cleavage of the pajamas, at the peeping breasts, and thought he saw age. He stared at her and through her with all the accumulated curiosity of ten thousand years. She was disturbingly attractive, provocative: Gregg Hodgkins couldn't have helped himself. (Hodgkins and how many others?) Only a human misogynist could have turned his back on her.

Nash leaned against the doorsill. "It's been a long time, Carolyn. What's new in old Egypt?"

She laughed at him, laughed at the double meaning to his feeble joke. "Sit down, Gilbert." She patted the divan beside her. "Sit down here."

He looked at her gun and her body. "No."

The laughter vanished. "I really expected something better of you than a cliche."

Nash said, "I'm tired."

"Has that girl worn you down?"

"You've worn me down. I've been chasing after you for some six or seven thousand years."

"And *now* you've caught me."

"And now I've caught you."

"Oh, sit down!"

He studied her a moment longer, studied her eyes and the expression on her face, the gun in her hand and the stage she had set for him. Nash turned away. He pulled out a straightbacked chair from under a small dining table and sat down there. A meal had been prepared for him and he examined that with interest: a nicely browned steak still sizzling on its platter, a half dozen attractive and aromatic side dishes, and a large slice of hot pie. At his elbow an electric percolator ceased its mad bubbling and shut itself off. In all, it was much more than he could possibly eat although he hadn't touched food since the previous evening—since Hoffman had fixed a meal.

Nash examined every dish on the table.

"A nice touch," he said. "Homey."

"Aren't you hungry, Gilbert?"

"You know damned well I am." A tight humorless grin appeared on his face. "I'm starving."

"Then eat it!" she said impatiently. "I prepared it for you when I saw you on the hill; I knew you had found me, I knew you would come down."

"I'm *sure* you prepared it for me. Only for me."

She came stiffly erect to frown at him. "Don't be silly. Why would I want to kill you?"

He glanced down at the gun. "Why, indeed?"

Carolyn held the frown, half angry at his dry insinuation. She became aware that her gaze had drifted to the table and quickly forced her attention back to him. "Aren't you going to eat it? I went to a lot of trouble for you, Gilbert."

"Irony, Carolyn?"

"Please! Let's not quarrel—not *us*. It has been too long a time and we are the only ones left. Please, Gilbert— Friends?"

Nash moved aside the steak platter and propped an elbow on the table. "All right, we're friends—for a little while. How are you, Carolyn?"

"Quite well, thank you. And you?"

"Quite well."

And they lapsed into silence. Nash kept his gaze on the woman, on her hands and body, on the way she sat on the divan. He watched for a sudden tenseness or a stiffening of the seemingly relaxed body, watched for muscle movement in her arms or hands. Almost lazily, he dropped his chin into the palm of his hand and let the savory odors from the table tease his nostrils. He wondered if there was cyanide in the coffee, or arsenic in the apple pie—it was difficult to guess which she would choose. After a while he blinked.

"Let's talk," she suggested uneasily.

"Let's," Nash agreed. "But about what?"

"We can talk while you eat."

"No, we can't. Bad manners."

"Stop it! Let's talk about us—and the others. Gilbert, do you realize how long it has been? We are the only ones left alive, aren't we? I'm *so* glad I found you—that you found me. Gilbert, it was terrible; there were times when I wanted to kill myself to escape the terrible loneliness. I've never been so alone." Her hands were moving restlessly in her lap, striking her knees to emphasize the points, but the gun always managed to remain pointed at him. "I'm so very glad you lived!"

He said, "Likewise."

"Did you have trouble?"

"Yes, in the beginning. A pack of wild little men wanted to stick me for a pig but I disappointed them; I managed to outdistance them. I think they had me marked for a meal, I think they were cannibals."

"But what of your wife? I seem to remember her?"

"She died in an earthquake," he answered without visible emotion. "Lisbon, 1755. We hadn't been together for very long."

"Oh." A moment of thoughtful silence. "And the others? There must have been others?"

Nash blinked again, sampling the aroma of apple pie and deciding *that* was the dish. "There were a few, yes. Do you remember Kero? Master electrician on the first deck? You don't remember him? I found him in Tuscany only about five hundred years ago—he had adopted some early-day scholar with an inquisitive mind and was trying to teach the man how to build and fly a ship. It didn't work—the scholar just couldn't get it through his head that a vessel *could* navigate in space, so Kero converted the ship to a submarine and the old man was delighted. He *could* understand that." Nash shook his head with regret. "Kero drowned trying to show the old man how it worked. Seaworthy subs can't be made of wood."

"That was very foolish."

Nash said, "And there was Raul. You *do* remember Raul? Ship's doctor? He died a short while ago in Egypt, a *very* old man—died happy, you might say. He had set himself up in the priesthood in the very early days, and stayed with it until that kind of priest went out of fashion. He was the officiating priest who married Ramses to that Hittite princess—I can't recall her name, but the marriage made history I understand. Raul took pleasure in that." Nash raised his gaze from the gun to the woman's eyes. "Raul was the first to tell me about you. He had heard stories drifting up from the south of Africa and we speculated on who might be causing them." He closed one eye to stare at her with the other. "*Some* stories."

She made no answer.

"And there was Santun, the second officer. He was the only fool in the lot—he committed suicide in a Roman arena. Santun fancied himself a devil with the ladies— perhaps you know that—but he was lacking in good judgment; when he realized he was marooned here for the rest of his life he ran wild. The poor devil woke up one morning to find himself with an incurable disease, and deliberately chose a violent, spectacular death in the arena to a slow and inglorious one in bed—alone. Raul and I were unwilling witnesses."

She said only, "I knew him."

"Next, there was Lef, the geologist—he had come out of the wreck with one eye missing but with a touch of belligerency to replace it. I had the devil's own time tracking *him*, piecing *his* story together. Lef had the misfortune to fall into a blizzard in the north country—his first winter there was almost his last, as well. But he grew to like it, I suppose, for he stayed there and eventually married. After several years he outfitted an expedition and sailed across the Atlantic searching for other survivors—searching for *us*. It was again his misfortune that he sailed in the wrong direction. He reached this continent, and vanished. I never caught up to him."

Nash suddenly shifted in his chair, turning his back on the table and the inviting food. Carolyn was watching him with a sly smile.

"I also discovered a girl named Brunna—did you know her? I suppose not." Nash let his eyes close to shut out the sight of the woman on the divan. "Brunna was a mechanic; she was on station aft, but was blown clear of the ship without injury. She had an interest in anthropology—it was something of a hobby with her. Can you guess where I found Brunna? In the mountains behind Afghanistan, searching for the source of life of *these* people, searching for the beginnings of human life. A starting point for humanity, a pinpoint of origin." He spread his hands in a half-circle to encompass the trailer court, the city below them and the world beyond. "She seemed to believe she had found it, in a place they call Tibet. Are you interested in all this?"

She nodded, but Nash didn't bother to open his eyes.

"Brunna and I enjoyed each other's company. I hadn't yet discovered my wife in Portugal, hadn't yet found her among the living, and so Brunna and I were seriously considering marriage when she fell into trouble. She was caught up by the soldiers of some Minoan king, and given alive to a lion. She was fed to the beast to appease some legendary lion-goddess." His eyes snapped open to glare at Carolyn Hodgkins. "The goddess was a bloodthirsty bitch. Brunna died because of her."

The silence came between them again.

After a while Carolyn asked, "Was that all? Just those few, and you and I?"

"If there were others they put up no signal."

"I would have *liked* seeing them again. Those poor few, those pitiful few."

"You were busy being a white goddess."

She looked at him, betraying no emotion.

Nash snapped his fingers with sudden memory. "Oh, there *was* someone else! Perhaps more than one, I don't know—I wasn't able to learn much. *Someone* introduced a form of writing to one of the old civilizations, one of the old tribes now long gone; a degenerate form of that writing still existed when I arrived there—it was changed, rather broken, but still readable after a fashion. I never found the originator. It was none of those I knew, none of those I've mentioned—but for a little while there was someone else, I think. You?"

"Not I."

"Not you, then. I've been quite interested in you, Carolyn —as was Raul while he lived. When I could, I followed your trail over most of the world although I didn't always know your identity. When I finally reached southern Africa you were already long gone, and your little empire there blown away with the winds of time; here and there a trace lingered, but only a trace—a religion can wither pretty quickly when the goddess gets tired and deserts her temple. By the time I returned to the Mediterranean you had also been *there,* but had moved on again. But *there* you had left a few little things behind which hadn't blown away with the winds; *there* many traces of your pseudo-religion stayed on."

"The bull," she said softly.

His hard stare bored into hers. "The dances, the bulls and the lions, the sacrifices and the feasts of blood—all those things were known to me. I knew where they came from, I knew which world spawned them, I knew how they were introduced to the tribes of *this* planet. Very few of our ship's company had ever visited the blood world that originated those games."

She didn't reply, but watched him.

"Some queer mementos of your passing turned up in Crete, in Palestine, in Egypt—ah, Egypt! In my library up the road I have a pornographic caricature of you. I don't think you would forgive the artist for what he did to you, but you might be amused at the pose. I don't know whether to compliment you, or him, for an extremely vivid imagination.

"But I never caught up to you, never found you; so *much* time passed without my finding you that at last I felt you were dead, I thought perhaps you *had* died in one of the plagues, or an earthquake, or in the fires that used to level those old cities. I had really given you up for dead—until the rocket experiments began in Germany. They were strong clues to your existence. I suspected you might be behind the experimentation.

"I very nearly caught you in Germany, Carolyn. It may have been only a matter of weeks—or days—when I missed you that time. I had reached Peenemunde. But when I heard of the theft of the forty-five quarts of water during *that* war, I realized I was too late; I knew you had gone, but I guessed where you were going. So—I followed you here. No—to be accurate, I preceded you here and tried to prepare for your coming. I've been waiting *here* for several years." He blinked at her. "And here we are. I wish I could say I was pleased to see you again."

"Yes, old mule, here we are. I wondered how much time you would take to get around to that." She sat up tall and stretched, moving her legs in provocative signal. "Just you and I, the last two sane people alive in a world of filthy savages. And so . . . ?"

"And so we have come together for a brief moment in time. Make the best of it, Carolyn. It won't last."

"Are you threatening me, mule?"

He lifted his head to stare at a point above her head, to stare into the distant past. "Raul said you were too evil to live."

"Raul was a meddling old fool!" she retorted.

"Raul," he contradicted, "was the oldest and wisest man I've ever known. His memory of our people and our kind of life went back well before my father's time, and perhaps *his* father as well. He said you were evil, and I accepted that judgment. He said you had lost all regard for life—other people's lives, the lives of these mortals you call filthy savages; he said that you had learned to kill or cause death at a whim, to maim and punish and destroy as it pleased you. And I've found that to be true. The misery and death and destruction you've caused cannot be denied—you are as unsane as *these* people and their penchant for continual wars. You caused Brunna's death; you killed Gregg Hodgkins; and you killed again yesterday." His hard stare locked with hers. "Raul gave me a commission. I accepted it."

There was a tiny, frozen smile on her lips. The gun was now at attention, aimed at his heart.

"*You* are playing the judge, old mule?"

He shook his head. "You haven't been listening, Carolyn. I said that Raul was the older and wiser man; *he* was your judge and *he* passed sentence. I accepted his judgment and I accepted his commission."

"To do what?"

"To stop you."

Carolyn Hodgkins rose up from the couch with one swift, lithe motion, coming to her feet in a startled reaction to his words. The gun hand stretched out toward him, and then was lowered in the following moment of doubt and indecision.

"I could stop *you* now, mule!"

"Perhaps."

"I could!" She glared at him with anger, and then in a moment attempted to regain a measure of self control. "Oh, Gilbert—Gilbert! Let's not quarrel. Not *us*. We are the only two left, we must stay together. Gilbert, a ship will be ready to fly in a very short while—we can go home again! We can go home together."

"Hodgkins's ship?"

"My ship," she contradicted. "*I* helped to build that ship at the Cape, *I* helped design it and power it, *I* put together the communications system that is the heart of it. Listen to me, Gilbert Nash: I prostituted myself with a pack of ignorant, stinking savages for more than a quarter-century to get that ship built—I lived with them, submitted to them, catered to them, fed them and educated them. I crammed knowledge and discovery into their miserable, ignorant heads until I was sick at the very sight of their hairy bodies, sick of their petty stupidities and their prattling gibberish; I fed them technical data until every one of them could fly a ship with his eyes closed and his hands bound; I coaxed them, teased them, flattered them, educated them, *forced* them to build a ship and a reaction motor for me. *I* wanted to go home again—and I will."

"You, alone?"

"Yes, if you persist in being stubborn."

Nash studied her for long, silent minutes.

He said finally, "I've decided how to stop you."

"You *aren't* going to stop me. Not now."

A tight grin. "I'm going to let them stop you, Carolyn. The dirty stinking little savages will do it."

"No, old man. I've planned better than that."

He was still grinning. "I'm going to let you commit

suicide, Carolyn. Raul would be satisfied with that—he would find a bit of grisly humor in it."

She laughed at him then, a husky raucous laughter that filled the trailer with mocking noise and seemed to echo from the walls. "Noble mule! Do you really think, noble old mule, that I'm about to commit suicide? Like Santun, perhaps? Exit in a blaze of glory while the savages applaud? Do you seriously believe I will throw myself away after all these years, after the work and the prostitution? Do you believe that, Gilbert?"

He waited until she had stopped. "Yes."

"But the Roman arenas are long gone!"

A shrug. "That ship is still on the pad."

"Forgetful mule! You've forgotten my profession."

"No, indeed. I know your skills."

"Then I am going."

"Perhaps. Want to shake on it and find out?"

She was quickly wary. "Explain that, Gilbert."

"Let's shake hands—or even better, enjoy a long farewell kiss for old times' sake. Let's pretend we are both ten thousand years younger—and then I'll tell you what I read."

"No! Oh, no! You would lie."

Nash grinned. "I promise not to lie. Let's find out, Carolyn. Let's carefully examine your future."

She sat down suddenly on the divan, attempting to put that much more distance between them. Her free hand was clenched, the other curled tightly about the gun. The small noises of the trailer court were audible around them.

She said at last, "*No.*"

"I've won, Carolyn."

Gilbert Nash inched his chair away from the small table and put his hands on his knees. It was a casual maneuver of a man who had decided not to eat after all, a man stretching out his arms to relax his muscles. He thought they were nearing the end of the joyless reunion and he wanted room to move when she made her decision.

He said, "You'll go alone; you have no intention of taking me along. You couldn't afford to take me back with you, Carolyn. I'd talk. I'd embarrass you." The yellow eyes held her fixed. "I'd tell sorry stories—and then you wouldn't be allowed to stay *there*, either."

"I'll go alone," she agreed brittlely. "You deserve to rot on this world. But I will pay glowing tribute to your memory, old mule—yours, and poor little Brunna, Santun, Lef, even Raul. You will be heroes, dead heroes buried in lost graves on a stinking ball of mud. They will not come searching for your graves, not when I am done with my story. Oh, it will be a memorable day when I reach home again, old man."

"*If* you reach home."

"Do you still doubt my ability, you poor fool? I can pilot that ship!"

"That ship will be controlled from base, from the Cape. It will be programmed for a planned voyage."

"You are a very stupid man, Gilbert. That ship will go where I will; that ship was designed to obey me. The savages don't know what they built into that ship."

He asked curiously, "Can you tap the repeaters?"

"Of course."

"And broadcast a distress signal?"

"Elementary."

"Can you override the telemetric controls?"

"Certainly! I *said* it was designed to obey me." She leaned forward, studying him, trying to guess at his intention. "Once off the pad that ship is mine to do with what I please; I can *take* it off the pad if need be. You *know* it won't be difficult to establish contact with our own people again, once that ship is up. Don't play at stupidity, old mule."

"You seem to have thought of everything."

"I've had ten thousand years to think."

"Food and water?"

"They will be on board."

"*Water?*"

"That reaction motor is jacketed with tanks of deuterium oxide—twice as much as it possibly needs."

He nodded in admiration. "Neat." He watched her hands. "You almost make me want to go along."

"I'm sure I will miss you, Gilbert."

"Of course you will—for a little while. But you will be a suicide."

"Stop being a stupid fool! Who knows that ship better, you or me?"

"You do."

"Then why do you keep saying that?"

"Because I think that. Want to kiss me?"

"*No.*"

"You'd find out why I think that. Carolyn, don't you know anything at all about these people and their passion for secrecy? Don't you know how well their installations are guarded? They fear their own citizens as much as they fear agents of other countries—they don't trust anyone. Radar will see you first and flash a warning to the patrols—or the fence will sense you and signal an alarm. Their fences are rigged to signal if a coyote wanders near, or a snake crawls under them." Nash grinned at her with feigned amusement and probed for an answer. "Or will you simply drive up to a gate and show a pass to the guards?"

Carolyn regarded him with distaste. "A slovenly mule as well as a stupid one. You've lived with these savages so long you think like they do. Peenemunde was well guarded too, fantastically well guarded; that madman's police shot people out of hand for simply being near the place, and yet I once stood twenty feet away—on the arm of an officer—and watched the assembly of a firing mechanism while the rocket lay in its cradle."

He said, "I believe you."

"The bold and open approach is the successful one. I won't have to worry about radar, I won't have to crawl under a fence, I won't have to *sneak* in, old mule. I've had several years to prepare other identities."

Nash let his jaw drop. "Hodgkins *said* you took long vacations from him, without him. He *said* you would disappear for months—and he thought you were in Florida, or California." He let his wonder stand on his face. "What kind of role do you play?"

She laughed at him, laughed at his seeming stupidity. "These savages like to believe their strength lies in their secrecy; they won't believe it is a weakness. *You* know their weaknesses, old man. How else have you moved around so freely?"

"I can't get onto the Cape to see a launch."

"I can!" she boasted. "As you say, I will simply drive up to the gate and show my pass."

"Airtight? Leakproof?"

"My other identity? Certainly. It is as solid as the ship I'm going to take into space."

"Well, I'll be damned!" The suspicion hit him and he stared at her with genuine wonder. "Carolyn, are you—did you—"

She said flatly, "I am on the same payroll as that man Dikty, as that man Cummings. Do you understand what their silly passion for secrecy has done to them, mule?"

"All of you are lodge brothers!" he exclaimed.

Carolyn said with cold satisfaction, "I helped organize the lodge more than thirty years ago. A woman they now believe to be dead was instrumental in setting up the Manhattan Project, in contributing to a special corps to guard the Project—and to guard all the other byproducts stemming from Manhattan right down to my ship. I have the necessary pass, Gilbert. I'm *in*."

Nash stood up and stepped away from the table. The food was turning cold.

"Carolyn, you're a wonder—and you're too much for me. It's time to go."

She leaped to her feet and raised the gun, holding it at arm's length like an amateur and aiming at his eyes. "No, you aren't leaving. I'm not going to let you ruin my chances now—not *now*, after this long."

"I won't talk about you, Carolyn. That's a promise. Go on and do whatever—"

She cut him off brusquely. "I can't afford your promises; I won't believe you." Her finger caressed the trigger. "My one hope of life is sitting down there on the pad now, waiting for me; my first real chance in ten thousand years is there for the taking. I'm not about to wait another ten thousand, old man. No more risks. I'm going and you are staying—here, in this trailer."

"Through the mouth?" he asked quietly. "Like your last husband?"

"Through the gut, if you prefer."

They faced each other, tense and waiting. With a growing inner tension Carolyn tightened the grip on the trigger. Nash dropped his gaze from hers to watch the trigger finger, knowing she would jerk it rather than squeeze off the shot.

He said quietly, "I don't want to be the last man out of the crew." A hand reached behind him.

"You won't be."

Nash jumped. Not at her—not as she expected, but sideways toward the door. His body hit the screen with a resounding thud and the booming explosion of the gun in the small trailer was like a thundering echo. He had hurled the coffee cup, and Carolyn jerked on the trigger when the cooling liquid splashed her face. The cup struck her chest and dropped to the floor.

She fired a wild second shot because she hadn't yet gained control of herself, and the picture tube of the television set imploded with another dull thunder.

Nash tumbled through the doorway and fell on the crushed rock of the nearby drive, staining it red. A man shouted in some adjoining cabin, and someone screamed. The trailer court was suddenly alive with people.

Chapter 13

ETHER AND FLOWERS.

The flowers were pink roses, a large bunch of them standing in a yellowed vase. The vase rested on a window sill and beyond the sill were the graceful swaying tops of trees, of blue summer sky. A face hung somewhere near the roses and the window, hung over the back of a chair, a face which smelled of ether and pink roses. Nash squinted at it, blinked and looked again.

Cummings said, "It's about time."

He sat on a chair that had been turned about, staring at the bed. His arms were folded across the chair top and his face seemed to be resting on his arms.

"Good morning," Nash said to the face. He looked at the blue sky beyond the window. "Good afternoon?"

"Good afternoon," Cummings reported. "You certainly took your time about it."

"Sorry to have troubled you," Nash said weakly.

"People around here are a little worried."

"About me?" Nash guessed.

"About you. Something about nonconformity."

"I was afraid of that," Nash confessed.

"I'm also concerned with the same, very much concerned."

There was a faint note of bitterness to his voice. "But I have to wait; the damned doctors hold jurisdiction here. I'm generously allowed fifteen minutes when you wake up."

Nash tried to nod. "*When* I do."

"You haven't yet. My fifteen minutes haven't started. And so I'm concerned about this nonconformity. People here are somewhat upset by a double heart and a double circulatory system. They fail to understand the absence of a vermiform appendix. One or two of them were extremely agitated over the activity or inactivity of certain endocrine glands." Cummings pursed his lips. "Now me, I'm not too much bothered by details like that because they don't mean much to me. The details are only that—details, added to the whole. The nonconformity of the whole puzzles me." The head moved on the crossed arms, peering at the man on the bed.

"I'll probably disappoint you," Nash replied, "but I can't help it or explain it. That's the way it *is*."

"That's the way *what* is?"

"Whatever you're talking about."

Cummings fell silent for a moment, and then tried a different tack.

"Wife took a shot at you, eh?"

"Not my wife."

"No. My apologies. Sister, maybe?"

"No relation—for which I'm thankful."

"Where did she go?" Cummings asked then.

"I didn't have time to watch," Nash retorted dryly. "Things moved rather fast last night."

"Last night?" The face hanging over the chair lit up in amusement. "Last night was eighteen days ago."

"*What?*"

"Eighteen days ago. You seem to have been out of touch

with the world; maybe I'd better bring you up to date. You lack a complete ear now, you know, and a bit of your skull. On the other hand you've gained a silver plate—back there." He indicated a spot on the side of his head. "Oh yes—and you had a mouthful of crushed rock. That must have been quite a farewell party last night. It all added up to eighteen days."

Nash burst out with, "Did the—?"

"Did the what?" Cummings followed curiously.

"Nothing."

"Did the *something*," the other persisted. "Did the woman get away from us again? Yes she did. We don't seem very efficient, do we? Did the trailer-court proprietor raise hell? Yes, he did; you frightened away some of the tenants. Did the farm boy up the hill tell us the story about your ditched car? Yes, he did—he went up to have a look for himself and the location was wrong. Did the what?"

"Did the lady take her trailer with her?"

"The lady took nothing but the clothes on her back—if she was dressed. Was she?" he asked curiously. "It would make a nice love nest for the newspapers." He considered that for a moment. "That's what they're printing, you know."

"Indeed?"

"Indeed, I didn't consider it fitting that they should pry into our affairs—so, the love nest. There was some loose talk of a rape charge against you."

Nash laughed weakly and found that it hurt.

Cummings shushed him. "Our fifteen minutes haven't started yet. You aren't awake?"

"Thanks." He looked toward the window. "Roses?"

"Hoffman."

"Nice girl."

"Useless girl. Thanks to you."

"I'm sorry—really am."

"She went in head over heels."

"I suspected that, and intended to stop it."

"Why?" Cummings asked candidly.

"Hell," Nash said, "I'm old enough to be her grandfather!"

"Oh, I don't know," the supervisor said quietly. "Not more than sixty-something, according to your police papers."

"All right then, father."

"I'd judge about thirty, looking at you."

"I feel like an old man."

"My friend," the agent said confidently, leaning forward, "you're going to feel one hell of a lot older when I get through with you! When this hospital releases you. One hell of a lot older!"

"Cheerful prospect," Nash assured him. "Makes me want to get out of bed now."

"Oh, take your time, take your time. Relax and enjoy yourself, let the pretty nurses wait on you. It'll be your last rest for a long, long time, my friend. I'm going to put you through the works, I promise you!" The head remained motionless over the back of the chair, but a smile appeared, a hollow, ghastly smile. "I'm going to ask questions and you're going to answer them—believe me, you'll answer them. You'll start by telling me where you came from and why. You'll tell me how and where you landed in this country, and when. You'll furnish minute detail of each and every hour of your life from the moment you were born until 'last night' eighteen days ago when an ambulance driver picked you up off the ground. You'll tell me your exact purpose for being here and exact reason for locating in this city. You'll tell me everything you know about the woman who married Gregg Hodgkins, why she married him, what her connection is to you, and why the two of you conspired to murder him. You'll tell me why the two of you murdered Dikty, why the two of you finally quarreled and she attempted to murder you. You'll tell me why the two of you were interested in the Ridge, why she married Hodgkins, why Hodgkins came to you, what he said to you. My friend," Cummings promised, *"you'll talk!"*

There was a clatter of quick steps and a flurry of white at the door. A young nurse put her head in to discover Nash awake. "Well! And how is our patient?" She glanced at her watch. "My, but you've been sleeping." She threw a fast glare at Cummings. "Why didn't you call me?" Back to Nash. "Do you want anything? Resting comfortably?" Again to Cummings. "I think you'd better leave now. You should have called me." And finally to Nash. "How are you?"

He answered, "Hello," and let it go at that.

Cummings tried to explain. "He just a minute ago woke up. He said to me—"

"I *thought* I heard voices in here," the nurse broke in. "I'll call the doctor. He'll be delighted to hear this." Another glare across the room. "You'd best leave, sir." Once more the man on the bed received her professional inspection. "Do you want anything?"

"No." He moved his head to grin at Cummings. "So long, chum, see you in the morning, no doubt."

"And the afternoon, *and* the evening, *and* the next morning after that, forever and ever. Don't forget what I said—I meant it all!" The supervisor got up from the chair to reveal that a body, after all, was attached to the balancing head. "I'll be here." He crossed over to the door and paused, turning again to look at Nash. "And *just* in case you're entertaining ideas, forget them. You'll find us in the corridor and all around the building." He made a circling motion with his finger.

Nash listened to his fading footfalls outside.

"Is there a man waiting in the corridor?" he asked the nurse.

"Yes sir."

"And outdoors too?"

"I think so. I haven't seen them, but some of the girls were talking."

Nash nodded. "Nurse—there *is* something I want."

"I thought so!" she grinned triumphantly, and opened a closet door to bring out a pan. "Visitors can be a nuisance at times." She came toward him.

"No, not that!" he protested.

The ready grin faded. "But I thought—"

"Sorry you misunderstood me. I want information, a newspaper. What's been happening?"

"Well, I'll try to find one." The grin returned to her youthful face. "You were in them—with a mysterious blonde. It's always a mysterious blonde, isn't it?" She stood off to examine him. "What did you do to her?"

"Nothing," he declaimed with mild exasperation, "and I'm not interested in mysterious blondes. Was there anything in the papers about a rocket ship—a space ship?"

"A space ship? Well—no. Should there be?"

"Are you sure? Nothing at all?"

"I didn't see anything." The nurse considered him for a moment. "Is it going to the moon or something?"

"I don't think so," Nash replied absently, slowly, his thoughts elsewhere. "I don't know, I can only guess. But I doubt very, very much that it's going to the moon. I don't think it was intended for the moon—" he broke off, looked up at the nurse. "May I have a glass of milk? And the papers?"

"Yes, sir." She came nearer to the bed and lowered her voice. "That policeman is quite angry with you. He's been storming up and down the corridor for days, just waiting. I hope you haven't done anything wrong. He seems to be making a lot of fuss just over a mysterious blonde."

"That policeman," Nash said, "wants to know the answers to a thousand questions—that's why he's angry with me. And do you know what? If I can't find a way out, a way to evade him and his men outside, I'll just have to stay and answer the questions." He grinned at the girl. "And don't think that won't add to his misery."

Chapter 14

GROUND ZERO:

The warning signals sounded for the last time and fell silent. From one of the observation posts a voice began the countdown—a voice multiplied over scores of loudspeakers on the Cape and literally millions of TV and radio speakers across the land. Vapors resembling live steam vented from the carrier rocket. Other than frightened, swooping birds and the vapors there was no visible movement or sign of life near the launch pad. The first atomic powered carrier was poised to hurl a survey ship into deep space.

Cameras mounted on vertical tracks aimed their lenses at the object; microphones were already storing small sounds on tape; a chase plane was circling and waiting a few miles away.

The object was a two-step carrier and instrument cabin.

The lower half of the vehicle was a liquid-fueled rocket of conventional design, a squat and powerful booster built solely for the purpose of getting the bird safely off the ground and to a height where a more efficient but potentially dangerous motor could assume the load. The booster was expendable and would be thrown away when its fuel was spent and when the stage next above could fire without fear of contamination. Later experimentation might show the liquid boosters to be an unnecessary precaution but this was a first and so the extra step was taken to protect the Cape and that part of the world around it.

The second stage was atomic powered, and would drive an instrument package beyond the solar system; it was designed to accompany the package to a nearby star system, circle it, and then drive the package home again before separating and hurling itself into the sun. Long before it returned home other and more sophisticated atomic rockets would go pounding into the skies to do a multitude of chores but this was a first and so it would be commanded to separate and throw itself away.

The instrument cabin at the very top of the vehicle would be returned to earth: it alone was not to be wasted. Later cabins would be enlarged to carry observation teams and life-support systems.

A sighing wind blew across the Cape, a hot wind from the interior blowing itself out to sea. Television crews from the networks waited impatiently alongside a distant road, many of them counting aloud with the firing officer. The highway was jammed with traffic.

Ignition:

Red-yellow fire scorched the concrete base below the vehicle and boiling steam raced down the waterway below the pad. Steam and smoke boiled up, threatening to obscure sight of the launch. Hoses fell away from the booster, dribbling liquid, and the sleek rocket began to climb away from between the gantries. It gave the illusion of staggering at the very beginning of a slow rise.

One hundred feet:

The beautiful monster continued to climb, gaining speed with every pound of spent fuel hurled from its belly. Tongues of fire continued to beat toward the ground, licking at the concrete and at the steel frames which had supported the bird. The robotic cameras climbed their vertical ladders to peer at the object, while the tapes recorded a mushrooming thunder of noise. Heatwaves from the underbelly again created the illusion of wobble, but the range safety officer calmly watched his instruments without comment or movement.

One thousand feet:

Climbing steadily, climbing fast; the bellowing lashes of fire no longer reached the ground, and the great noise of the bird's passage registered a fraction of a second late on the mechanical ears and the tapes left behind. The air around and behind the vehicle boiled with heat and flame but still the beautiful ship climbed without fault, pushing its load into the sky. The chase plane circled near, ready to follow the bird to its own uppermost limit.

Ten thousand feet:

Up, always up, with no more illusion of wobble or hesitation. The cameras strained at the top of their tracks but could do no more than scan several degrees of morning sky, seeing only a smoky trail and seeing the chase plane dart away in hot pursuit. The more mobile television cameras followed the ship across the sky, creating a new illusion that it was flying on its back. The high, thin smoke trail wavered as it was caught in moving air currents and soon lost its shape. The last of the thunderous noises of passage had come, been caught on tape, and were heard no more.

Human eye and glass lens would soon lose sight of the hurtling object.

Fifteen miles:

The first stage suddenly fell silent—dead—as the fuel tanks drained themselves dry; the eruption of fire, smoke and thunder ceased abruptly as the rocket motor stopped its heavy pounding. The task of the first stage was complete and now it waited passively for abandonment. In the instrument cabin, sensors noted the empty tanks and obediently tripped a relay. Shrouds and braces connecting the first and second stages blew away, fired by explosive bolts, and measured seconds later small jet motors thrust the hulk away from the upper body of the ship. Staging was completed, and the lifeless booster seemed to drift backward from the climbing rocket. There seemed to be no other activity for many long minutes. The ship climbed in silence.

Fifty miles:

Instruments in the cabin and on earth noted a minute deflection in the line of flight. Flight officers stared with astonishment at the readings flowing into the operations room, at the tell-tale meters showing activation of the atomic motor in the second stage long before that activity was due. The bird was accelerating, when it should have been coasting toward a parking orbit. Another deflection was noted, a new line of flight that would carry the ship wide of its programmed target.